LONGMAN IMPRINT BOC

CW01011196

Stories frc _ _ _

···

Voices and themes of African cultures

Selected and edited by Madhu Bhinda

General editor: Michael Marland
Series consultant: Geoff Barton

LONGMAN

Longman Imprint Books
General editor: Michael Marland

New titles
Characters from Pre-20th-Century Novels selected and
   edited by Susie Campbell
Diaries and Letters selected and edited by Celeste Flower
Genres selected and edited by Geoff Barton
Highlights from 19th-Century Novels selected and edited by Linda Marsh
Landmarks selected and edited by Linda Marsh
Scenes from Plays selected and edited by Michael Marland
Stories from Africa selected and edited by Madhu Bhinda
Stories from Europe selected and edited by Geoff Barton
Ten Short Plays selected and edited by Geoff Barton
Travel Writing selected and edited by Linda Marsh
Two Centuries selected and edited by Geoff Barton

Previously published titles
Autobiographies selected and edited by Linda Marsh
Black Boy Richard Wright
Cider with Rosie Laurie Lee
The Diary of Anne Frank edited by Christopher Martin
Ghost Stories selected by Susan Hill
The Human Element and other stories Stan Barstow
I'm the King of the Castle Susan Hill
P'tang, Yang, Kipperbang and other TV plays Jack Rosenthal
A Roald Dahl Selection edited by Roy Blatchford
Stories from Asia selected and edited by Madhu Bhinda
Strange Meeting Susan Hill
The Woman in Black Susan Hill

For CB, Suresh and Jayashree

Contents

Introduction   v

Map of Africa   viii

West Africa

The Late Bud   1
by Ama Ata Aidoo (Ghana)

Marriage is a Private Affair   13
by Chinua Achebe (Nigeria)

The Ivory Dancer   21
by Cyprian Ekwensi (Nigeria)

A Man Can Try   31
by Eldred Durosimi Jones (Sierra Leone)

Ding Dong Bell   38
by Kwabena Annan (Ghana)

Northern Africa

The Answer Is No   49
by Naguib Mahfouz (Egypt)

Another Evening at the Club   53
by Alifa Rifaat (Egypt)

The Story of the Chest   62
by Marguerite Amrouche (Algeria)

Central and Southern Africa

No Witchcraft for Sale   68
by Doris Lessing (Zimbabwe)

The Advance   78
by Henry Lopes (Congo)

The Ultimate Safari   87
by Nadine Gordimer (South Africa)

Kgotla   101
by Bessie Head (South Africa)

East Africa

The Return   112
by Ngugi Wa Thiong'o (Kenya)

The Rain Came   119
by Grace Ogot (Kenya)

Study activities   132

The authors   146

Further reading   150

Introduction

Africa has made a major contribution to literature in English. Vast and varied, Africa is the second largest continent, having a quarter of the world's land surface. Its 550 million people make up more than 11 per cent of the world's population, living in forty-nine countries. There are over 3000 different ethnic groups and over 1000 languages. Several countries have more than one indigenous language and these usually coexist with an official language, the language of the former colonial power, which is not the first language of the majority. Indeed, many people will not be able to speak, read or write it. The most widespread religions are Christianity and Islam.

For all this diversity there is a strong sense of Africa among all its peoples, and this has never been felt so strongly. As one of the authors in this collection, Doris Lessing, puts it:

> I believe that the chief gift from Africa to writers, white and black, is the continent itself . . . Africa gives you the knowledge that man is a small creature among other creatures, in a large landscape.

The people of Africa celebrate their unity as well as their diversity.

There is a massive range of arts across Africa, some of which have not been much known in other continents, although there have been centuries of contact and influence. The arts of ancient Egypt have been well known across the world and in this century modern African poetry and drama have been very widely appreciated.

Fiction has become a major African art with novels by African writers being read across the world, and since the

1950s the short story has developed and become established as a widely written and read literary genre. The practical merits of the short story as an art form may partly explain its popular success in Africa: it can take less time to write than a novel and it is more cheaply and quickly published, initially in magazines. The possibilities of the short story as a means of commentary by the author suggest another reason for its success: the turmoils of many countries as they struggled out of colonialism led to social conflicts and the wish of writers to comment.

It is obviously difficult to define 'African literature' because it is not the literature of a country but of a very diverse continent. Should you include all writers who were born in Africa, even if they are white and their ancestors moved there in fairly recent times? Should you include Africans who have moved away and live and write in other countries? Most European literatures are defined in terms of the languages in which they are written. The definition of African literature is further problematic because of its many languages: the languages of the European colonisers, English, French and Portuguese; Arabic in the north; Swahili in Kenya and Tanzania and numerous African languages. Ngugi Wa Thiong'o is one of those who have insisted that African literature has to be written in an African language. His own story in this book, because he wrote it in English, he would call part of 'Euro-African' literature. Of the fourteen stories, ten were originally written in English. The stories of Mahfouz and Rifaat from Egypt were translated from Arabic, while those of the Algerian Amrouche and the Congolese Lopes were translated from French.

This collection is of stories by writers born and living (from their early lives at least) in Africa, usually writing in English, but they are from nine different countries from the north, south, east and west, and from different language and ethnic backgrounds. They are stories from and about Africa.

There is little point in agonising about definitions, but they all meet Nadine Gordimer's description:

> One must look at the world *from Africa,* to be an African writer, not look *upon Africa* from the world.

The stories describe the lives of people outside the central spotlights of the history of Africa's nations. Personal and family events are the core of almost all of them. Yet what happens to these ordinary people is usually heavily influenced by the wider public history. Their story is part of their country's history. Their loves, care of their children, family relationships, working lives and social lives are influenced by the background of colonialism in Africa, one of the recurrent African short-story themes: we see this very powerfully tackled in *A Man Can Try.*

South African writers are often concerned with issues of race and conflict and with differences of material resources as well as political status and power between people, and how these affect their lives.

The status of women and the feminist point of view are treated with astonishing brevity and force by two Egyptian writers: in *The Answer Is No* by Mahfouz and *Another Evening at the Club* by Rifaat. In Egypt the issue of women's rights has had to struggle with conservative social customs. Authors in North Africa, particularly women writers, frequently focus on the role and status of women in Islamic patriarchal societies.

The wars of Africa are a painful aspect of many stories. The forced movement of people as a result of war is the subject of Nadine Gordimer's *The Ultimate Safari,* and war and its consequences are also featured in *The Return* by the Kenyan Ngugi Wa Thiong'o.

West Africans, however, seem to have been relatively free from the turmoils and tensions of these other regions and tend to focus on more local African cultural themes and issues. There is, therefore, a perceptible general difference of tone between stories from different regions and this is one reason why the Contents page is grouped by region. Compare, for instance, the difference of tone between *The Late Bud* from Ghana with *The Advance* from the Congo: both stories involve relationships between mothers and their children, but the feelings they arouse in the reader are very different because the societies they are set in determine what possibilities exist for individual human action.

The short story has been a major form in Africa and the short stories from Africa have become one of the world's great literary strengths.

Madhu Bhinda

The Late Bud

by Ama Ata Aidoo

'The good child who willingly goes on errands eats the food of peace.' This was a favourite saying in the house. Maami, Aunt Efua, Aunt Araba ... oh, they all said it, especially when they had prepared something delicious like cocoyam porridge and seasoned beef. You know how it is.

First, as they stirred it with the ladle, its scent rose from the pot and became a little cloud hanging over the hearth. Gradually, it spread through the courtyard and entered the inner and outer rooms of the women's apartments. This was the first scent that greeted the afternoon sleeper. She stretched herself luxuriously, inhaled a large quantity of the sweet scent, cried 'Mm' and either fell back again to sleep or got up to be about her business. The aroma did not stay. It rolled into the next house and the next, until it filled the whole neighbourhood. And Yaaba would sniff it.

As usual, she would be playing with her friends by the Big Trunk. She would suddenly throw down her pebbles even if it was her turn, jump up, shake her cloth free of sand and announce, 'I am going home.'

'Why?'

'Yaaba, why?'

But the questions of her amazed companions would reach her faintly like whispers. She was flying home. Having crossed the threshold, she then slunk by the wall. But there would be none for her.

Yaaba never stayed at home to go on an errand. Even when she was around, she never would fetch water to save a dying soul. How could she then eat the food of peace? Oh, if it was a formal meal, like in the morning or evening, that was a different matter. Of that, even Yaaba got her lawful share.... But not this sweet-sweet porridge. 'Nsia, Antobam, Naabanyin, Adwoa, come for some porridge.' And the other children trooped in with their little plates and bowls. But not the figure by the wall. They chattered as they came and the mother teased as she dished out their titbits.

'Is yours all right, Adwoa? ... and yours, Tawia? ... yours is certainly sufficient, Antobam.... But my child, this is only a titbit for us, the deserving. Other people,' and she would squint at Yaaba, 'who have not worked will not get the tiniest bit.' She then started eating hers. If Yaaba felt that the joke was being carried too far, she coughed. 'Oh,' the mother would cry out, 'people should be careful about their throats. Even if they coughed until they spat blood none of this porridge would touch their mouths.'

But it was not things and incidents like these which worried Yaaba. For inevitably, a mother's womb cried out for a lonely figure by a wall and she would be given some porridge. Even when her mother could be bile-bellied enough to look at her and dish out all the porridge, Yaaba could run into the doorway and ambush some child and rob him of the greater part of his share. No, it was not such things that worried her. Every mother might call her a bad girl. She enjoyed playing by the Big Trunk, for instance. Since to be a good girl, one had to stay by the hearth and not by the Big Trunk throwing pebbles, but with one's hands folded quietly on one's lap, waiting to be sent everywhere by all the mothers, Yaaba let people like Adwoa who wanted to be called 'good' be good. Thank you, she was not interested.

But there was something which disturbed Yaaba. No one knew it did, but it did. She used to wonder why, every time Maami called Adwoa, she called her 'My child Adwoa', while she was always merely called 'Yaaba'.

'My child Adwoa, pick me the drinking can.... My child you have done well....'

Oh, it is so always. Am I not my mother's child?

'Yaaba, come for your food.' She always wished in her heart that she could ask somebody about it.... Paapa ... Maami ... Nana, am I not Maami's daughter? Who was my mother?

But you see, one does not go round asking elders such questions. Take the day Antobam asked her grandmother where her own mother was. The grandmother also asked Antobam whether she was not being looked after well, and then started weeping and saying things. Other mothers joined in the weeping. Then some more women came over from the neighbourhood and her aunts and uncles came too and there was more weeping and there was also drinking and libation-pouring. At the end of it all, they gave Antobam a stiff talking-to.

No, one does not go round asking one's elders such questions.

But Adwoa, my child, bring me the knife.... Yaaba ... Yaaba, your cloth is dirty. Yaaba, Yaaba ...

It was the afternoon of the Saturday before Christmas Sunday. Yaaba had just come from the playgrounds to gobble down her afternoon meal. It was kenkey and a little fish stewed in palm oil. She had eaten in such a hurry that a bone had got stuck in her throat. She had drunk a lot of water but still the bone was sticking there. She did not want to tell Maami about it. She knew she would get a scolding or even a knock on the head. It was while she was in the outer room looking for a bit of kenkey to push down the troublesome bone that she heard Maami talking in the inner room.

'Ah, and what shall I do now? But I thought there was a whole big lump left.... O ... O! Things like this irritate me so. How can I spend Christmas without varnishing my floor?'

Yaaba discovered a piece of kenkey which was left from the week before, hidden in its huge wrappings. She pounced upon it and without breaking away the mildew, swallowed it. She choked, stretched her neck and the bone was gone. She drank some water and with her cloth, wiped away the tears which had started gathering in her eyes. She was about to bounce away to the playgrounds when she remembered that she had heard Maami speaking to herself.

Although one must not stand by to listen to elders if they are not addressing one, yet one can hide and listen. And anyway, it would be interesting to hear the sort of things our elders say to themselves. 'And how can I celebrate Christmas on a hardened, whitened floor?' Maami's voice went on. 'If I could only get a piece of red earth. But I cannot go round my friends begging, "Give me a piece of red earth." No. O ... O! And it is growing dark already. If only my child Adwoa was here. I am sure she could have run to the red-earth pit and fetched me just a hoeful. Then I could varnish the floor before the church bells ring tomorrow.' Yaaba was thinking she had heard enough.

After all, our elders do not say anything interesting to themselves. It is their usual complaints about how difficult life is. If it is not the price of cloth or fish, then it is the scarcity of water. It is all very uninteresting. I will always play with my children when they grow up. I will not grumble about anything. . . .

It was quite dark. The children could hardly see their own hands as they threw up the pebbles. But Yaaba insisted that they go on. There were only three left of the eight girls who were playing *soso-mba*. From time to time mothers, fathers or elder sisters had come and called to the others to go home. The two still with Yaaba were Panyin and Kakra. Their mother had travelled and that was why they were still there. No one came any longer to call Yaaba. Up till the year before, Maami always came to yell for her when it was sundown. When she could not come, she sent Adwoa. But of course, Yaaba never listened to them.

What is the point in breaking a game to go home? She stayed out and played even by herself until it was dark and she was satisfied. And now, at the age of ten, no one came to call her.

The pebble hit Kakra on the head.

'*Ajii.*'

'What is it?'

'The pebble has hit me.'

'I am sorry. It was not intentional.' Panyin said, 'But it is dark Kakra, let us go home.' So they stood up.

'Panyin, will you go to church tomorrow?'

'No.'

'Why? You have no new cloths?'

'We have new cloths but we will not get gold chains or earrings. Our mother is not at home. She has gone to some place and will only return in the afternoon. Kakra, remember we will get up very early tomorrow morning.'

'Why?'

'Have you forgotten what mother told us before she went away? Did she not tell us to go and get some red earth from the pit? Yaaba, we are going away.'

'*Yoo.*'

And the twins turned towards home.

Red earth! The pit! Probably, Maami will be the only woman in the village who will not have red earth to varnish her floor. *Oo*!

'Panyin! Kakra! Panyin!'

'Who is calling us?'

'It is me, Yaaba. Wait for me.'

She ran in the darkness and almost collided with someone who was carrying food to her husband's house.

'Panyin, do you say you will go to the pit tomorrow morning?'

'Yes, what is it?'

'I want to go with you.'

'Why?'

'Because I want to get some red earth for my mother.'

'But tomorrow you will go to church.'

'Yes, but I will try to get it done in time to go to church as well.'

'See, you cannot. Do you not know the pit? It is very far away. Everyone will already be at church by the time we get back home.'

Yaaba stood quietly digging her right toe into the hard ground beneath her. 'It doesn't matter, I will go.'

'Do you not want to wear your gold things? Kakra and I are very sorry that we cannot wear ours because our mother is not here.'

'It does not matter. Come and wake me up.'

'Where do you sleep?'

'Under my mother's window. I will wake up if you hit the window with a small pebble.'

'*Yoo.* . . .We will come to call you.'

'Do not forget your *apampa* and your hoe.'

'*Yoo.*'

When Yaaba arrived home, they had already finished eating the evening meal. Adwoa had arrived from an errand it seemed. In fact she had gone on several others. Yaaba was slinking like a cat to take her food which she knew would be under the wooden bowl, when Maami saw her. 'Yes, go and take it. You are hungry, are you not? And very soon you will be swallowing all that huge lump of fufu as quickly as a hen would swallow corn.' Yaaba stood still.

'*Aa.* My Father God, who inflicted on me such a child? Look here, Yaaba. You are growing, so be careful how you live your life. When you are ten years old you are not a child any more. And a woman that lives on the playground is not a woman. If you were a boy, it would be bad enough, but for a girl, it is a curse. The house cannot hold you. *Tchia.*'

Yaaba crept into the outer room. She saw the wooden bowl. She turned it over and as she had known all the time, her food was there. She swallowed it more quickly than a hen would have swallowed corn. When she finished eating, she went into the inner room, she picked her mat, spread it on the floor, threw herself down and was soon asleep. Long afterwards, Maami came in from the conversation with the other mothers. When she saw the figure of Yaaba, her heart did a somersault. Pooh, went her fists on the figure in the corner. Pooh, 'You lazy lazy thing.' Pooh, pooh! 'You good-for-nothing, empty-corn husk of a daughter ...' She pulled her ears, and Yaaba screamed. Still sleepy-eyed, she sat up on the mat.

'If you like, you scream, and watch what I will do to you. If I do not pull your mouth until it is as long as a pestle, then my name is not Benyiwa.'

But Yaaba was now wide awake and tearless. Who said

she was screaming, anyway? She stared at Maami with shining tearless eyes. Maami was angry at this too.

'I spit in your eyes, witch! Stare at me and tell me if I am going to die tomorrow. At your age ...' and the blows came pooh, pooh, pooh. 'You do not know that you wash yourself before your skin touches the mat. And after a long day in the sand, the dust and filth by the Big Trunk. *Hoo! Pooh!* You moth-bitten grain. *Pooh!*'

The clock in the chief's house struck twelve o'clock midnight. Yaaba never cried. She only tried, without success, to ward off the blows. Perhaps Maami was tired herself, perhaps she was satisfied. Or perhaps she was afraid she was putting herself in the position of Kweku Ananse tempting the spirits to carry their kindness as far as to come and help her beat her daughter. Of course, this would kill Yaaba. Anyway, she stopped beating her and lay down by Kofi, Kwame and Adwoa. Yaaba saw the figure of Adwoa lying peacefully there. It was then her eyes misted. The tears flowed from her eyes. Every time, she wiped them with her cloth but more came. They did not make any noise for Maami to hear. Soon the cloth was wet. When the clock struck one, she heard Maami snoring. She herself could not sleep even when she lay down.

Is this woman my mother?

Perhaps I should not go and fetch her some red earth. But the twins will come....

Yaaba rose and went into the outer room. There was no door between the inner and outer rooms to creak and wake anybody. She wanted the *apampa* and a hoe. At ten years of age, she should have had her own of both, but of course, she had not. Adwoa's hoe, she knew, was in the corner left of the door. She groped and found it. She also knew Adwoa's *apampa* was on the bamboo shelf. It was when she turned and was groping towards the bamboo shelf that she stumbled over the large water-bowl. Her chest hit the edge of the tray. The tray tilted and the water poured on the floor. She could not rise up. When Maami heard the noise her fall made, she screamed 'Thief! Thief! Thief! Everybody, come, there is a thief in my room.'

She gave the thief a chance to run away since he might attack her before the men of the village came. But no thief rushed through the door and there were no running footsteps in the courtyard. In fact, all was too quiet.

She picked up the lantern, pushed the wick up to blazing point and went gingerly to the outer room. There was Yaaba, sprawled like a freshly killed over-grown cock on the tray. She screamed again.

'Ah Yaaba, why do you frighten me like this? What were you looking for? That is why I always say you are a witch. What do you want at this time of the night that you should fall on a water-bowl? And look at the floor. But of course, you were playing when someone lent me a piece of red earth to polish it, eh?' The figure in the tray just lay there. Maami bent down to help her up and then she saw the hoe. She stood up again.

'A hoe! I swear by all that be that I do not understand this.' She lifted her up and was carrying her to the inner room when Yaaba's lips parted as if to say something. She closed the lips again, her eyelids fluttered down and the neck sagged. 'My Saviour!' There was nothing strange in the fact that the cry was heard in the north and south of the village. Was it not past midnight?

People had heard Maami's first cry of 'Thief' and by the time she cried out again, the first men were coming from all directions. Soon the courtyard was full. Questions and answers went round. Some said Yaaba was trying to catch a thief, others that she was running from her mother's beating. But the first thing was to wake her up.

'Pour anowata into her nose!' – and the mothers ran into their husbands' chambers to bring their giant-sized bottles of the sweetest scents. 'Touch her feet with a little fire.' ... 'Squeeze a little ginger juice into her nose.'

The latter was done and before she could suffer further ordeals, Yaaba's eyelids fluttered up.

'*Aa*.... *Oo* ... we thank God. She is awake, she is awake.' Everyone said it. Some were too far away and saw her neither in the faint nor awake. But they said it as they trooped back to piece together their broken sleep. Egya Yaw, the village medicine-man, examined her and told the now-mad Maami that she should not worry. 'The impact was violent but I do not think anything has happened to the breast-bone. I will bind her up in beaten herbs and she should be all right in a few days.' 'Thank you, Egya,' said Maami, Paapa, her grandmother, the other mothers and all her relatives. The medicine-man went to his house and came back. Yaaba's brawniest uncles beat up the herbs. Soon, Yaaba was bound up. The cock had crowed once, when they laid her down. Her relatives then left for their own homes. Only Maami, Paapa and the other mothers were left. 'And how is she?' one of the women asked.

'But what really happened?'

'Only Benyiwa can answer you.'

'Benyiwa, what happened?'

'But I am surprised myself. After she had eaten her kenkey this afternoon, I heard her movements in the outer room but I did not mind her. Then she went away and came back when it was dark to eat her food. After our talk, I went to sleep. And there she was lying. As usual, she had not had a wash, so I just held her ...'

'You held her what? Had she met with death you would have been the one that pushed her into it – beating a child in the night!'

'But Yaaba is too troublesome!'

'And so you think every child will be good? But how did she come to fall in the tray?'

'That is what I cannot tell. My eyes were just playing me tricks when I heard some noise in the outer room.'

'Is that why you cried "Thief"?'

'Yes. When I went to see what it was, I saw her lying in the tray, clutching a hoe.'

'A hoe?'

'Yes, Adwoa's hoe.'

'Perhaps there was a thief after all? She can tell us the truth ... but ...'

So they went on through the early morning. Yaaba slept. The second cock-crow came. The church bell soon did its Christmas reveille. In the distance, they heard the songs of the dawn procession. Quite near in the doorway, the regular pat, pat of the twins' footsteps drew nearer towards the elderly group by the hearth. Both parties were surprised at the encounter.

'Children, what do you want at dawn?'

'Where is Yaaba?'

'Yaaba is asleep.'

'May we go and wake her, she asked us to.'

'Why?'

'She said she will go with us to the red-earth pit.'

'O ... O!' The group around the hearth was amazed but they did not show it before the children.

'*Yoo*. You go today. She may come with you next time.'

'*Yoo*, Mother.'

'Walk well, my children. When she wakes up, we shall tell her you came.'

'We cannot understand it. Yaaba? What affected her head?'

'My sister, the world is a strange place. That is all.'

'And my sister, the child that will not do anything is better than a sheep.'

'Benyiwa, we will go and lie down a little.'

'Good morning.'

'Good morning.'

'Good morning.'

'*Yoo*. I thank you all.'

'So Maami went into the apartment and closed the door. She knelt by the sleeping Yaaba and put her left hand on her bound chest. 'My child, I say thank you. You were getting ready to go and fetch me red earth? Is that why you were holding the hoe? My child, my child, I thank you.'

And the tears streamed down her face. Yaaba heard 'My child' from very far away. She opened her eyes. Maami was weeping and still calling her 'My child' and saying things which she did not understand.

Is Maami really calling me that? May the twins come. Am I Maami's own child?

'My child Yaaba . . .'

But how will I get red earth?

But why can I not speak . . .?

'I wish the twins would come . . .'

I want to wear the gold earrings . . .

I want to know whether Maami called me her child. Does it mean I am her child like Adwoa is? But one does not ask our elders such questions. And anyway, there is too much pain. And there are barriers where my chest is.

Probably tomorrow . . . but now Maami called me 'My child!' . . .

And she fell asleep again.

Marriage is a Private Affair

by Chinua Achebe

'Have you written to your dad yet?' asked Nene one afternoon as she sat with Nnaemeka in her room at 16 Kasanga Street, Lagos.

'No. I've been thinking about it. I think it's better to tell him when I get home on leave!'

'But why? Your leave is such a long way off yet – six whole weeks. He should be let into our happiness now.'

Nnaemeka was silent for a while, and then began very slowly as if he groped for his words: 'I wish I were sure it would be happiness to him.'

'Of course it must,' replied Nene, a little surprised. 'Why shouldn't it?'

'You have lived in Lagos all your life, and you know very little about people in remote parts of the country.'

'That's what you always say. But I don't believe anybody will be so unlike other people that they will be unhappy when their sons are engaged to marry.'

'Yes. They are most unhappy if the engagement is not arranged by them. In our case it's worse – you are not even an Ibo.'

This was said so seriously and so bluntly that Nene could not find speech immediately. In the cosmopolitan atmosphere of the city it had always seemed to her something of a joke that a person's tribe could determine whom he married.

At last she said, 'You don't really mean that he will object to your marrying me simply on that account? I had always thought you Ibos were kindly disposed to other people.'

'So we are. But when it comes to marriage, well, it's not quite so simple. And this,' he added, 'is not peculiar to the Ibos. If your father were alive and lived in the heart of Ibibio-land he would be exactly like my father.'

'I don't know. But anyway, as your father is so fond of you, I'm sure he will forgive you soon enough. Come on then, be a good boy and send him a nice lovely letter . . .'

'It would not be wise to break the news to him by writing. A letter will bring it upon him with a shock. I'm quite sure about that.'

'All right, honey, suit yourself. You know your father.'

As Nnaemeka walked home that evening he turned over in his mind different ways of overcoming his father's opposition, especially now that he had gone and found a girl for him. He had thought of showing his letter to Nene but decided on second thoughts not to, at least for the moment. He read it again when he got home and couldn't help smiling to himself. He remembered Ugoye quite well, an Amazon of a girl who used to beat up all the boys, himself included, on the way to the stream, a complete dunce at school.

'I have found a girl who will suit you admirably – Ugoye Nweke, the eldest daughter of our neighbour, Jacob Nweke. She has a proper Christian upbringing. When she stopped schooling some years ago her father (a man of sound judge-ment) sent her to live in the house of a pastor where she has received all the training a wife could need. Her Sunday School teacher has told me that she reads her Bible very fluently. I hope we shall begin negotiations when you come home in December.'

On the second evening of his return from Lagos

Nnaemeka sat with his father under a cassia tree. This was the old man's retreat where he went to read his Bible when the parching December sun had set and a fresh, reviving wind blew on the leaves.

'Father,' began Nnaemeke suddenly, 'I have come to ask for forgiveness.'

'Forgiveness? For what, my son?' he asked in amazement.

'It's about this marriage question.'

'Which marriage question?'

'I can't – we must – I mean it is impossible for me to marry Nweke's daughter.'

'Impossible? Why?' asked his father.

'I don't love her.'

'Nobody said you did. Why should you?' he asked.

'Marriage today is different ... '

'Look here, my son,' interrupted his father, 'nothing is different. What one looks for in a wife are a good character and a Christian background.'

Nnaemeka saw there was no hope along the present line of argument.

'Moreover,' he said, 'I am engaged to marry another girl who has all of Ugoye's good qualities, and who ... '

His father did not believe his ears. 'What did you say?' he asked slowly and disconcertingly.

'She is a good Christian,' his son went on, 'and a teacher in a Girls' School in Lagos.'

'Teacher, did you say? If you consider that a qualification for a good wife I should like to point out to you, Emeka, that no Christian woman should teach. St Paul in his letter to the Corinthians says that women should keep silence.' He rose slowly from his seat and paced forwards and backwards. This was his pet subject, and he condemned vehemently those church leaders who encouraged women to teach in their schools. After he had spent his emotion on a long homily he at last came back to his son's engagement, in a seemingly milder tone.

'Whose daughter is she, anyway?'

'She is Nene Atang.'

'What!' All the mildness was gone again. 'Did you say Neneataga, what does that mean?'

'Nene Atang from Calabar. She is the only girl I can marry.' This was a very rash reply and Nnaemeka expected the storm to burst. But it did not. His father merely walked away into his room. This was most unexpected and perplexed Nnaemeka. His father's silence was infinitely more menacing than a flood of threatening speech. That night the old man did not eat.

When he sent for Nnaemeka a day later he applied all possible ways of dissuasion. But the young man's heart was hardened, and his father eventually gave him up as lost.

'I owe it to you, my son, as a duty to show you what is right and what is wrong. Whoever put this idea into your head might as well have cut your throat. It is Satan's work.' He waved his son away.

'You will change your mind, Father, when you know Nene.'

'I shall never see her,' was the reply. From that night the father scarcely spoke to his son. He did not, however, cease hoping that he would realise how serious was the danger he was heading for. Day and night he put him in his prayers.

Nnaemeka, for his own part, was very deeply affected by his father's grief. But he kept hoping that it would pass away. If it had occurred to him that never in the history of his people had a man married a woman who spoke a different tongue, he might have been less optimistic. 'It has never been heard,' was the verdict of an old man speaking a few weeks later. In that short sentence he spoke for all his people. This man had come with other to commiserate with Okeke when news went round about his son's behaviour. By that time the son had gone back to Lagos.

'It has never been heard,' said the old man again with a sad shake of his head.

'What did Our Lord say?' asked another gentleman. 'Sons shall rise against their Fathers; it is there in the Holy Book.'

'It is the beginning of the end,' said another.

The discussion thus tending to become theological, Madubogwu, a highly practical man, brought it down once more to the ordinary level.

'Have you thought of consulting a native doctor about your son?' he asked Nnaemeka's father.

'He isn't sick,' was the reply.

'What is he then? The boy's mind is diseased and only a good herbalist can bring him back to his right senses. The medicine he requires is *Amalile*, the same that women apply with success to recapture their husbands' straying affection.'

'Madubogwu is right,' said another gentleman. 'This thing calls for medicine.'

'I shall not call in a native doctor.' Nnaemeka's father was known to be obstinately ahead of his more superstitious neighbours in these matters. 'I will not be another Mrs Ochuba. If my son wants to kill himself let him do it with his own hands. It is not for me to help him.'

'But it was her fault,' said Madubogwu. 'She ought to have gone to an honest herbalist. She was a clever woman, nevertheless.'

'She was a wicked murderess,' said Jonathan who rarely argued with his neighbours because, he often said, they were incapable of reasoning. 'The medicine was prepared for her husband, it was his name they called in its preparation and I am sure it would have been perfectly beneficial to him. It was wicked to put it into the herbalist's food, and say you were only trying it out.'

Six months later, Nnaemeka was showing his young wife a short letter from his father:

> *'It amazes me that you could be so unfeeling as to send me your wedding picture. I would have sent it back. But on further thought I decided just to cut off your wife and send it back to you because I have nothing to do with her. How I wish that I had nothing to do with you either.'*

When Nene read through this letter and looked at the mutilated picture her eyes filled with tears, and she began to sob.

'Don't cry, my darling,' said her husband. 'He is essentially good-natured and will one day look more kindly on our marriage.' But years passed and that one day did not come.

For eight years, Okeke would have nothing to do with his son, Nnaemeka. Only three times (when Nnaemeka asked to come home and spend his leave) did he write to him.

'I can't have you in my house,' he replied on one occasion. 'It can be of no interest to me where or how you spend your leave – or your life, for that matter.'

The prejudice against Nnaemeka's marriage was not confined to his little village. In Lagos, especially among his people who worked there, it showed itself in a different way. Their women, when they met at their village meeting, were not hostile to Nene. Rather, they paid her such excessive deference as to make her feel she was not one of them. But as time went on, Nene gradually broke through some of this prejudice and even began to make friends among them. Slowly and grudgingly they began to admit that she kept her home much better than most of them.

The story eventually got to the village in the heart of the Ibo country that Nnaemeka and his young wife were a most happy couple. But his father was one of the few people in the village who knew nothing about this. He always displayed so much temper whenever his son's name was mentioned that everyone avoided it in his presence. By a tremendous effort of will he had succeeded in pushing his son to the back of his mind. The strain had nearly killed him but he had persevered, and won.

Then one day he received a letter from Nene, and in spite of himself he began to glance through it perfunctorily until all of a sudden the expression on his face changed and he began to read more carefully.

> '... Our two sons, from the day they learnt that they have a grandfather, have insisted on being taken to him. I find it impossible to tell them that you will not see them. I implore you to allow Nnaemeka to bring them home for a short time during his leave next month. I shall remain here in Lagos ...'

The old man at once felt the resolution he had built up over so many years falling in. He was telling himself that he must not give in. He tried to steel his heart against all emotional appeals. It was a re-enactment of that other struggle. He leaned against a window and looked out. The sky was overcast with heavy black clouds and a high wind began to blow filling the air with dust and dry leaves. It was one of those rare occasions when even Nature takes a hand in a human fight. Very soon it began to rain, the first rain in the year. It came down in large sharp drops and was accompanied by the lightning and thunder which mark a change of season. Okeke was trying hard not to think of his two grandsons. But he knew he was now fighting a losing battle. He tried to hum a favourite hymn but the pattering of large raindrops on the roof broke up the tune. His mind immediately returned to the children. How could he shut his door against them? By a curious mental process he imagined them standing, sad and forsaken, under the harsh angry weather – shut out from his house.

That night he hardly slept, from remorse – and a vague fear that he might die without making it up to them.

The Ivory Dancer

by Cyprian Ekwensi

A shadow fell across the table in the market stall and the girl behind the rows of candles, matchboxes and tinned provisions displayed on it looked up. Across the motor park a young man was striding briskly. It was Chibo and he did not pause as usual to chat with the drivers, to leave orders with the wine hawkers and make eyes at the bean sellers. He appeared to be in some haste, and was coming towards her stall.

She could not look at this splendid local youth without a feeling of guilt and remorse. In his simple yellow singlet and scarlet lappa,[1] he was every bit as manly and honest as any girl could desire. She could not deny that her parents had made a good choice, but she was afraid that after fifteen years, things were going wrong. No longer did she look upon their marriage as inevitable.

He did not smile. A few yards from the table, he paused and hitched up his lappa impatiently. 'Er ... Akunma, the Chief said I should call you ...'

'Ah, Chibo! Not even a smile! Why, is there something? Or is it just that –'

'No,' said Chibo. 'What else can there be? I was sent to call you and I've done so.' His eyes were hard.

'Mm! ...' sighed Akunma. 'I wonder what the Chief wants me for?'

[1] loin-cloth

21

'I don't know,' said Chibo. 'He saw me passing by and said: "Go to the market and call me the ivory dancer." And I came. Are you not the ivory dancer, the best dancer in the village of Nankwo?'

Akunma's eyes became coy. 'So they say ... but, if it is to do with dancing, er ... I promised someone ...'

'You mean Peters?' Chibo laughed. There was no joy in his laughter. 'But he's away, isn't he?'

'When he comes back, he'll know. You know how the girls of Nankwo run after him ... they'll do anything to get him.'

'That's fine!' said Chibo. 'Do you blame them? He's from the University, and he wears a rag round his neck and sees through pieces of broken bottles. His father talks of sending him to England. Why shouldn't all the girls, including you, my fiancée, run after him?'

'Chibo!' Her eyes glinted resentfully, but, as she arranged her head-tie her unsteady fingers betrayed her. 'You're just jealous, that's all. Look after the stall for me, please! Or are we such enemies now?' She pinched his forearm. 'I shan't be long.'

'Remember I have work on the farm. I'm not a college boy; I earn my living by hard work, not wearing glasses and ties!'

The Chief kept Akunma waiting long enough for her to count the number of rafters on the ceiling. This room where the elders met seemed to be decorated with the horns and skins of strange animals. And there were old clocks too, some of which had stopped ticking. Akunma was following the lazily swinging pendulum of the oldest one when the door opened abruptly.

Framed in the doorway stood a big man in a flowing cloth. His eyes fixed her in a drunken stare. She said, 'Long may you live' and knelt down respectfully before him, and he called her 'my daughter' and bade her rise.

'Rise, my daughter,' he said, walking into the middle of the room. 'I sent for you, because I want you to know that you will be dancing tonight ...'

'But, Chief –'

'What is it? Are you taking the words from my mouth? Is that all the training you've had?'

'Forgive me, Chief.'

He went on as if nothing had happened, but she could see that her interruption had annoyed him. This was the wrong thing to do to a man like Chief Nanka.

'Two important men are coming to this village tonight,' he said. 'Sir Ajumobi, our representative in the Senate, the highest government council in this country, is arriving today on a tour of inspection. For a long time now I have been pressing for good water supply for the village and nothing has happened. Now I want to reach the heart of this our son who has never been home since he became a wealthy and important man in Pitakwa fifteen years ago. I want to exhibit your dance tonight to impress him and get him to get the minister to give us water. Your dance is the best in these parts and will put him in the mood to listen to me. Besides Sir Ajumobi is bringing his friend, an American something, I don't know ... when he comes he'll tell us more about him. It is very important to me and the village that you dance your best. Do you hear me? Go now and gather your dance troupe together –.'

Akunma did not rise to her feet. 'Chief, can we not leave this till tomorrow?'

'Go and stop answering back to your seniors!'

'Chief, I beg you, listen! I made a promise to my ... my betrothed ... never to dance again in public –'

'Who? Chibo?' snarled the Chief.

'No, not him. I mean – Peters, the boy from college. You know him ...'

'The one who always puts on tie ... You let me lay my hands on him! ...'

'Er ... you know he has been spending his holidays here.'

'I don't know, no man in this village knows either. Only you women do! Now, go and gather your little girls before I use my authority.'

'Chief, when Peters came here, he took on a job as mechanic with one of those lorries ... the ones that go to the coal city every day and fetch coal for the steamers on the Niger ... he did that to show me he is a good boy. Now he is gone back to the coal city. His relatives live there and he is gone to consult them. This night they are coming back and will ask my mother for my hand. Oh, Chief! Do you not see that I must keep myself decent and respectable till everything is settled?'

'You are mad! In Nankwo here no one knows Peters. Chibo is the one we know you are betrothed to ... You cannot just throw him aside like that here! The elders must know. You are wasting your time, my girl. Leave this matter to me and your mother. Now go! There is little time between now and evening. In a moment, our guest and his friend will arrive.'

'Chief, I shan't do it! I shan't dance! ...' She was weeping now. The Chief glared at her for a moment before leaving the room. Akunma heard him talking in rage to his wives. She was afraid. This man was noted for his sheer wickedness. What had she done? What was she going to do now? Some moments passed. Everywhere was silent, yet she could sense a strange restlessness beneath.

A side-door opened. Two masked men came in. They took her by the wrists and led her, as gently as they could, to the back of the house. There was a sort of inner courtyard, lined on one side by a row of rooms from each of which a woman stared curiously out. This was the Chief's harem.

The masked men guided her to one of the rooms, pushed her in, and left. It was not an unpleasant room. It was well lighted, with an expensive-looking four-poster bed in one corner and a table lined with books in the other. The frocks which hung from pegs on the wall were well cut, and Akunma wondered whose room this might be. The door opened and a young lady in a smart frock came in. She was the Chief's youngest wife, and she was smiling.

'Mmm!' she said. 'So you are the girl! I thought as much! The Chief has sent me to persuade you to change your mind. It's a waste of time trying to be loyal to Peters! He's no good, that one. He's merely deceiving you. Just think of it! A boy who is going to be one of the country's leaders very soon ... what do you think he'll do with you?'

Akunma said: 'I know you are the right woman for him! Because you have been to St Anne's Convent. Isn't that so? But the Chief can't read or write properly, and yet he married you!'

'I'm here to help him,' she said. 'Though his other wives dislike me, I am not sorry.'

'You are selfish and wicked,' Akunma said. 'That's why it suits both of you. But I know that you are deceiving the Chief. One day, when you have saved up enough money, you are going to pack away all his goods and escape!'

'Nonsense! Don't talk to me like that!'

'What have you come to do?'

The Chief's wife sat on the bed. 'This is my room,' she said. 'But I came to tell you that the Chief is threatening to take away your mother's farm if you do not dance tonight. You know your mother ... how poor she is! Without that farm, she is useless! Of course, those Iroko trees which your father left behind ... the matter is still being debated. The Chief can still decide against you. But what does it all matter? So long as you have Peters, you can run away and leave your mother to starve!'

Akunma's head dropped. 'Wicked ... both of you ... very wicked.'

In a few hours, the Chief's wife had painted such a miserable picture that Akunma sat huddled in a corner of the room, a silent, helpless prisoner. Occasionally, a little girl came in with a garland of flowers. There were twenty girls in all who formed her troupe – splendid, graceful girls aged five to thirteen. They knew the movements in their most intricate form, and dancing was to them a never-ending source of joy. Seeing one of them come in, her anklets jingling, her body painted with camwood, Akunma knew the Chief would spare no pains to present this show to the Senator. What a scheming scoundrel he was! And while under the influence of the delightful spectacle, he would strike home, get a good water system for Nankwo, while she lost her best chance in life.

The Chief looked in at dusk. 'When are you going to start rehearsals? Is your troupe ready yet? What dance are you going to perform? Let it be the dance of the elephant, the one that earned you the name of the ivory dancer. That's the best of them all. Have you polished your ivory bangles yet?'

'She has been sitting in that corner, moping!' said the Chief's wife.

Akunma flared up. 'Leave me alone! Oh, why do things go against me in this way? Here in the village, they think I'm too sharp. Nobody wants me as a wife. Even Chibo is afraid of me. And when a decent man comes along . . .'

The Chief interrupted her. 'Shut your mouth! I've had enough of this! Since you are so obstinate, you'll force me to do what I don't like! When the Senator comes I'll tell him how your Peters killed a man on the road to the coal city. Can't help that now!'

'He . . . killed . . . a man?' Akunma stammered.

But the Chief had gone leaving the two women to themselves.

'So, you didn't hear of it?' the Chief's wife asked. 'It was all hushed up, of course. Your Peters was actually at the wheel, but to save him, the owner of the lorry took the blame and paid the fine. A very nice man. He didn't want them to know that Peters had no driving licence . . .'

'Do you mean that . . . Peters was responsible and not the other man? I heard of the accident. About a month ago. Just after Peters came to Nankwo.'

'You did not hear the truth.'

'Oh, Lord! I beg you . . . can't you tell the Chief to drop the matter? You know how he loves you . . . even made you head over much older women . . . please beg him not to dig up the past.'

'I am powerless,' the Chief's wife said. 'Unless, of course, you are prepared to dance?'

'No! . . . That's impossible! I would rather die!'

The sun had vanished behind the trees when the Pontiac, followed by a crowd of hooting boys, drove into the village. Sir Ajumobi, dressed in an impeccably cut dark-grey flannel suit, lit his pipe as he came out followed by the American who wore a light gabardine suit and a green-lined helmet.

'Sam Billings, the film producer,' he said introducing his friend, his expansive wave embracing the palm trees and the thatched huts under the banana groves. 'He's shooting a film on Africa and wants a dance sequence for a scene ... perhaps you have the answer here, Chief ...'

'Perhaps so!' The Chief sounded uncertain. 'And now ... er ... the Rest House is ready. I think you need a wash and change after that journey. Since you say you are leaving tomorrow morning I will try and arrange a dance for tonight. But it will not start before nine since the dancers would want time to prepare.'

The car moved towards the Rest House and the Chief went back at once to the courtyard and saw Akunma. But all the response he got was: 'I shall not break my word to Peters.'

'You'll have to dance if he doesn't come back before eight. It's seven now!'

Half an hour later Chibo brought back the market stall keys. He had sold a piece of cloth for twenty shillings. He was like that, always dependable.

'Akunma,' he said anxiously. 'It's all over Nankwo that you said you are not dancing. What is this foolishness?'

'It is nothing.'

'I beg you, Akunma. Whatever you do, think carefully. Chief is too dangerous for that.'

In the forest glade, the sweepers were clearing away the leaves that littered the dance square. Women arranged chairs and dusted up the lamps. In the Chief's senior wife's room, twenty young and graceful girls, scented and painted, were donning their anklets and bangles. Only Akunma remained aloof from the throbbing excitement that was stirring the village. Drums were sounding now.

The Chief's wives had assembled in front of her door and were chattering impatiently. Still Peters had not returned. Time was running out. The Chief's wives trooped away towards the glade, colourful and excited.

Every strange sound took Akunma to the door. And now her calm gave way to anxiety, and anxiety to a strange dread of what might happen to her if she failed the Chief. Along the path a party of old men hobbled, called, 'Akunma, where are you?'

Not long after the old men went by a youth, tattered, bruised and torn, broke into the room where Akunma was held prisoner. It was Peters.

'Oh!' exclaimed Akunma. 'What happened? Where are your relatives?'

'An accident ... Akunma, you must dance ... The Chief plans evil ... Dance, hear me? I permit you! Dance and save me!'

'What about ... seeing my people?'

'That can wait! Your people will be at the dance. Put on your ivory bangles. Dance! Don't be late!'

He hurried off. Akunma was trembling. Would she still be as supple and graceful as she used to be? The ivory bangles felt heavy on her wrists and her neck seemed too frail to support the bridal mask of the spirits. But when she entered the ring, her eyes were dancing with a thousand lights. The lightness returned to her feet as they wove intricate patterns on the ground. A forest of eager eyes followed her. She felt, rather than saw the important group under the mantle lamp: the Chief in the centre, Sam Billings sucking his cigar on one side, the Senator leaning over to shield a flame from the wind ...

Next morning, her limbs still ached. Her heart still fluttered with fear; anklets still tinkled in her ears. Sam Billings' encore topping the thunderous applause woke her dreams and plunged her back again.

Somewhere in front of the house she could hear Chibo's voice. She struggled out of bed. He had brought her a basket of fresh oranges and bananas from his farm. He praised her so lavishly that she concealed her initial disappointment at not seeing Peters. Only the fear of hurting him kept her from asking about Peters.

Chibo told how the Senator had promised to get them the long-needed pump water, but he feared that some people might not like to pay rates. He had also heard that Sam Billings, the film magnate, was arranging to put the ivory dancer into his film on Africa. And all because Akunma had shone last night.

'But I can't understand how some people act,' he said. 'I mean – that boy, Peters . . .'

Akunma held her breath. The smile vanished from her face. 'Peters?' she echoed. In the icy stillness her voice was scarcely audible.

'Yes . . . '

'Well, you were wasting your time! Last night, while you were dancing to save him, Peters and the Chief's most senior wife ran away together! No, don't waste your tears! It suits them . . . can't you look on the bright side?'

'Leave me for a while,' said the ivory dancer.

She did not wipe her tears or restrain her sobs as she walked back to the bed.

A Man Can Try

by Eldred Durosimi Jones

'Well, I think this is very satisfactory' – old Pa Demba, the Paramount Chief of Bomp, looked at D.C.[1] Tullock with genuine admiration. 'I think you have been very generous to Marie. I really do not see how anyone could have been fairer than you have been – one hundred pounds a year for Marie and a good secondary school education for the boy.' Pa Demba turned to Marie: 'You should count yourself lucky to have had D.C. Tullock for your husband. I have seen many girls who have lived with men like the D.C. for many years, only to be abandoned at the end without any provision. According to this paper, you and your child have been well provided for. And now you are free to marry anyone you wish. I am going to sign as a witness. Do you agree to the terms?'

As Marie nodded in dumb agreement the tears which had stood poised on the corners of her eyes rolled down her chubby brown cheeks. Tullock looked away through the open office window, and gazed unseeingly at the town beyond. The figure of Marie sitting there stroking the hair of her son Tambah, who stood between her knees, was to him a silent indictment. She sat scarcely moving except for her hands which moved so slowly and tenderly along the boy's head that

[1] District Commissioner – a senior British Government official in charge of an area

31

she looked perfectly still. She was like a statue of maternity – mother and child. Tullock thought, she and I have shared in the miracle of creation and here I am about to desert her and the boy. But he persuaded himself that it had to be, although even in the moment of decision he could not avoid condemning himself.

As for Marie, she just sat there stroking her little boy's hair – he had fine silky hair – she was glad that he resembled Tullock in that feature at least. She would always remember him by it. She felt no bitterness at Tullock's departure, only sorrow – intense sorrow. She had known from the first that this moment would come. In their type of relationship, parting was as inevitable as death; but like death, when it actually came, it was still something of a shock. She had served her turn with Tullock. They had been happy within the limits of their relationship for eight years. All the women had called her Marie Tullock, although there was no legal bond between them. Now, Tullock was leaving the service to join his father's law firm – the richer for his experience in Africa. Of course he could not take Marie with him. So he had devised this settlement.

In spite of his generosity by prevailing standards, Tullock felt rather cheap in his own eyes. For unlike some others in his position, he had the uncomfortable habit of judging everyone by a single standard. He could not have disentangled himself from a girl of his own race so easily. He knew this, and the very fact that he could shake off Marie without any complications with a gratuity of his own naming, made him ill at ease with himself.

He, too, had been happy with Marie, at least, quite content with her. She was pretty, cooked well, was affectionate but unobtrusive. True she couldn't read

Shakespeare – couldn't read anything at all in fact. The world situation left her completely unmoved, for she knew nothing about what happened outside the town of Bomp where she had lived all her life. In fact to quote Prothero – Old Prothero, the father of the provincial administration – 'a barbarian, a pretty barbarian, but a barbarian like the rest of them'. It was he who had helped Tullock solve his little problem, although he did not see what the fuss was all about. He saw no problem. He had laughed at Tullock's solemnity. 'Look, my boy!' he had said, with his hand on Tullock's shoulder, 'I've had a woman – and children – in every district I've worked in. The only rules are – never get your heart involved and never move with a woman from one district to another; creates no end of trouble. After each station, I just paid them off; no problem at all. Glad of the money they were, too. They were soon snapped up by the native burghers of the district. Don't let this worry you, Boy. Pay Marie off. She'll forget you soon enough. And as for you, once on the boat you'll soon forget about her.'

Tullock had secretly wondered how one who was so meticulous over jot and tittle of colonial regulations could be so casual over matters of the heart. But he checked his flow of self-righteousness. Who was he to judge anyway. He was no better than Prothero – in fact he was worse. For while Prothero had never thought his relationship with African women came within his ordinary moral code, he knew that what he was doing was wrong. He had, however, taken Prothero's advice and had arranged a settlement for Marie. He had taken infinite trouble to make it legal – an inadequate sop to his conscience – but he thought it was the least he could do. So here they were signing the agreement.

Pa Demba signed his name, rose and took his leave,

still commending Tullock's generosity. The three who were left sat on in silence. There seemed to be nothing to say. Tullock was overcome with shame, Marie with grief. Tambah was just bewildered. He knew his mother's tears were caused by Tullock but he did not know how.

'Well, Marie, this is good-bye.'

Marie's eyes welled, her bosom heaved, but she uttered not a sound. She had dreaded this moment almost as soon as she realised how much she liked the feel of Tullock's hair; how longingly she listened for the honk of his horn as he swerved madly into the compound from the office. In her moments of greatest happiness with him she had always felt the foretaste of this parting in her mouth. Now it was here.

'I have got the court messengers to take your things to your uncle's house. Good-bye, Marie; you know I have to go, don't you?'

Marie nodded and tried to smile. She turned suddenly to the door, grasped Tambah's hand and hurried away. Tullock watched her disappear down the drive without once turning to look back. He knew that a part of his heart had gone with her.

Trevor Tullock's decision to return home was not as sudden as it seemed – the reason had been on his mind for quite some time. He had been engaged for three years, to the daughter of his father's oldest friend – a London stockbroker. Only the omnivorousness of the human mind could have accommodated two such different women as Marie and Denise, even at different times. Marie, African, illiterate, soft and melting, was entirely devoted to Tullock – she lived only for him. Denise was English, sophisticated, highly educated and a very forward member of the central office of her political party. She was intensely alert and held strong convictions on almost every subject, particularly the rights of women. She had made it quite clear that she had no intention of leaving her life in England and burying herself in the wilds of Africa. She was too engrossed in what was going on in England. In her own country she was part of the scene. She was always addressing women's gatherings, organising demonstrations, canvassing on behalf of the party from door to door, and this sort of work she could not bear to leave. So Trevor had to make up his mind to return home if he wanted to marry her. He had put it off long enough already and had just been helped to make up his mind by a long pleading letter from home. 'What would people think?' his mother had pleaded ... So Trevor had decided that he could decently put it off no longer.

In the whirl of official farewells and the thousand and one things he had to do to catch the boat, Trevor Tullock had had little time to think of his future life. He had taken it all for granted. On the boat, however, he could not stop himself from thinking. But it was the image of Marie that kept coming to his mind, pushing out that of Denise – Marie sitting with Tambah between her knees. He did not think very much about the boy and even this worried him, for after all he was his own flesh and blood. He tried to shut off thoughts of Marie, but he found it difficult. He tried because he thought it was his duty. But he could not. He tried to drown his thoughts in drink, but that only made him morbid. He began to look forward to his arrival in England – England with its distractions and Denise!

Denise! This instrusion of Denise into his thoughts startled him. Now that he started thinking about her, doubts about their relationship came rushing into his mind. Doubts of the most fundamental kind. Did he really want to marry Denise? He brushed the question aside. It did not matter. He had to. So the boat bore him speedily along to a fate from which his mind equally speedily shrank.

At Liverpool, Trevor leaned over the rails and peered into the Mersey mist, trying to discern the faces of the visitors on the balcony. There was his mother and yes – beside her was Denise.

His mother waved enthusiastically and Denise put up her right hand in a jerky, almost official act of welcome. Her trim tweeded business-like figure, through sheer force of contrast, brought back the image of the brown, loose-robed, welcoming frame of Marie. His life with her had been relaxed and easy. His home life in Africa had been so dramatically different from his office life. He had never had to argue with Marie. He was always sure of her willing obedience. Denise, on the other hand, had a quicksilver mind. Life with her was a constant mental tug-of-war. That was in fact the very quality in their relationship which had so exhilarated him during their undergraduate days. Now, the thought of a lifetime with her gave him a chilly feeling. The change from one woman to the other was like the physical change he had just made – exchanging the warmth and relaxation of Africa for the chill, bracing air of England. That economical wave of Denise's, symbolic of her detachment and her control over herself, made Trevor realise with horrid clarity that while he had changed, she had not. How had he changed? He tried to think. He had not lost his love for books; he still read them though, now, with a less belligerent attitude towards their authors than before. No doubt Denise, with whom he had cut many an author to pieces, would say that he was less acutely critical; but he still enjoyed reading – probably even more than before. What else? He certainly drank more, and more often than before. His drinking action was now a hearty swallow compared with the old sip and savour of those rather pretentious wine-tasting parties. He was now more concerned with the contents of the bottle than with the suggestions on the label. No doubt Denise would say his palate had coarsened. The more he thought, the more Trevor saw that life with Denise would now have to be one long never-ending effort to live up to a life he no longer believed in ... 'till death us do part.'

He braced himself, picked up his bags, and strode down the gangway. 'A man can try,' he muttered to himself, already aiming a peck at Denise's proffered cheek.

Ding Dong Bell

by Kwabena Annan

Not having much development in our village, we all agreed when the Government Agent told us that we should do something about it. I remember the occasion very well. It was towards the end of March when the cocoa was all in, packed and sent to the coast, and Kwesi Manu had started his house again. Every year he would buy the cement, engage a couple of Northern Territories' labourers, lay out the blocks, and then run out of money. The walls had been built two years back; last year, he had managed to get the roof on, only to have it flung off again by the great Easter storm which did so much damage. The iron sheets were flung like a handful of pebbles across the street, knocking down Ama Serwah's stall. The old lady put Kwesi before the Native Authority Court for failing to pay for the loss, and this caused a first-class row which lasted us all through the rains.

The village certainly needed to be improved. The roads were laterite[1] tracks from which the dust rose like thunder clouds whenever a lorry went through the place. Goats, chickens and sheep wandered about its alleys and slept in the doorways. We were always complaining of the difficulty of getting supplies from the nearby town, and to hear the women grumble you would think that it was unusual to walk a mile or so to

[1] clay

fetch water from the pool. Still, we accepted the life; it had been lived a long time, as we all knew, and if there had been nothing to complain of we might have quarrelled much more often among ourselves than we do now.

We hadn't any local council either. The chief was well liked, and we saw no reason to change. There had been talk of joining us up with the next village to form a 'local authority area'. The Government Agent was always on about it. But our neighbours were a grasping lot, always farming our land and trying to claim that it belonged to them, and we preferred our separate existence. I suppose it was this that made the Government down in Accra[2] take up the idea of development. If we wouldn't join in a local council, it was because we were too set in our ways, and 'development' would get us out of them. We understood all that. But when the Government Agent asked us whether we agreed to anything, we always said yes. It was easier in the long run to agree and never did any harm. And as a matter of fact, on this occasion, we forgot all about the idea until one Wednesday morning when the chief beat 'gong gong' to call us together. When we reached the palace there was our chief, *Nana*, and an educated clerk sitting in the compound. I call him 'educated' because he was obviously a town man, in neat city clothes, with a black book under his arm and pencils sticking in his hair. It turned out that he was a new clerk in the Government Agent's office and had been sent to talk to us.

We listened to what he had to say, although we had heard most of it before: how we should think again about forming a local council, how we should pay the

[2] capital of Ghana

levy on time, why didn't we help the local teacher and send our children to the mission school, did we not know that the Government had forbidden the making of *akpeteshie*[3] because it was dangerous to drink, why had we not cleared the bush right down to the river. It was much like the regular routine visit, which kept the Government satisfied and left us alone, with the local Native Authority policeman standing there ready to walk round the village looking for *akpeteshie,* and having a quiet drink of it with the clerk behind the court-house – until the clerk suddenly told us that the Government Agent had been so pleased when we had asked for his help that he was sending a Development Officer the following week to make a start.

We didn't quite know what to make of this, and it soon slipped our memory – the next day being Thursday when we don't farm, and a good week's supply of liquor is ready for use. I had business to do in Kumasi the following weekend – I usually stock up with a few cases of corned beef and sardines for the store – and did not get back until late on Wednesday morning. The first thing I saw in the village was a large black car with pick-axes. The whole village had turned out to see what it was all about, and as I came up a tall thin European in blue shorts and shirt was standing in front of the crowd lecturing them. He couldn't speak our language *twi* of course, but you could have told just by the way he waved his arms that he meant business. The chief looked as pleased as he could, but I could see that he was worried, and the elders sat in stony disapproval.

'Great changes are taking place in the country,' the European said, through a rat-faced interpreter. 'Last

[3] an alcoholic drink

week I was in Accra and everywhere I could see great buildings going up, good roads, good schools. And what can be done in Accra can be done too in the villages.'

Well, I could have told him straight away that he was making a mistake. The one thing we detest hearing about is Accra and what the city crooks are doing with our money. Then before anyone could stop him, he was off about our neighbours: how co-operative they were, how ready they had been for his help, how they said they were going to extend the lorry park and the market. ('So that they can put their prices up,' shouted a voice, but this voice was hushed down.) Then he got on to us. He was worried about the water and the roads. Of course we agreed. If you ask anybody in our town whether this or that is good, you will always be told that everything is as bad as it can be. We don't boast and we like to grumble. So by the time the European had asked us about the latrines and the roads and the rains, and whether the harvest was good, and how we liked the new mission school, he must have thought we were ready for all the development there was in the country.

The only time he got stuck was when he suggested that we line the streets with deep concrete gutters, and Tetteh Quarshie stood up and said no, that wouldn't do, he must have somewhere for his ducks to get food and drink. The European didn't quite know whether to take this seriously or not – and Tetteh stood there, bent with age and drink, clutching his cloth to his bony ribs and muttering like someone from the Kumasi asylum – so he left it and came to the point (which all of us could see he had fixed on long before he set foot in the town).

There was nothing wrong with the idea in theory. We were to dig out two or three wells by the forest path leading to the main road with the help of some 'well-diggers', and a mason who knew how to case the sides with special concrete rings. We might have to dig twenty or thirty feet down, but there were plenty of rings and, when we were finished, the water in each well would stay sweet throughout the year. It took a long time to explain, but most of us soon grasped the idea. Only, we don't care to do things in a hurry. So the chief spoke for us all when, after politely thanking the officer for his trouble, he told him that we would discuss it and let the Government Agent know our decision. Up came little Francis Kofi with a basin of eggs which Opanin Kuntor handed to the clerk with a second round of thanks. And before the European knew what was happening, the meeting had broken up and he was being led to his car. Off it went in a cloud of dust, followed by the Land Rover, and we settled down again.

After this, of course, the letters began to arrive – Your good friend this, Your good friend that; His Honour was anxious to hear what we had decided; Could we agree to Monday week for the diggers to make a start?; and so forth. We sat quiet and said nothing. There is no post office in our town, and the effort of getting stamps and paper is usually enough to deter the chief from correspondence.

Monday came and went, so did Tuesday and Wednesday; and on Thursday we collected as usual at Kofi's bar. By three in the afternoon, we had started on the *akpeteshie*, and at half-past four no one noticed the arrival of the Government Agent and his car until he sent his clerk stumbling and sweating down the road to ask for *Nana* and the elders.

'He is not well,' said Kofi Tandoh.

'He has travelled.'

'He is mourning for his sister.'

'He has the measles.' This came from a young idiot of a schoolboy who had edged his way into the group.

The clerk stood first on one leg, then on the other, and scratched his head. He knew as well as we did that after half a bottle of *akpeteshie* the chief might as well have travelled for all the help he could give. I believe the clerk said as much to the Government Agent, a fattish European with a red face and pale eyes, who immediately flew into a rage, cursed the chief and the village, and then ordered the constable with him to go and seize the still[4] and what was left of the liquor. But he was unlucky. We usually have two or three kerosene tins cooling off in Opanin Kuntor's yard, but this time, with the cocoa season over and a good number of funerals under way, we were down to a few bottles only. By the time he had collected these, and we sat there without raising a finger in apology or protest, *Nana* himself appeared. He was far from normal and came roaring out of the palace apparently thinking that he was celebrating the yearly *adae* festival.[5]

The Government Agent gave him one look and drove off without a word. We all went back to sleep. But the next morning we were worried. We had a hurried meeting at the palace, brought in the schoolmaster to advise, and agreed that something must be done to turn away the wrath to come. The only way seemed to be 'development'. So we sent Francis Kofi on a bicycle with a letter drawn up by the teacher, with *Nana* and the elders making their mark.

It seemed to meet the case, for two days later the Land Rover came back, with the European. The site was cleared and we took it in turns to dig. It was easy work

[4] apparatus for making *akpeteshie*
[5] new harvest festival, held in July

and unmarred by any mishap, except on the second night the European was with us when old Nyantechie went out before the moon rose to obey the call of nature, stumbled over one of the concrete rings and pitched into three feet of well. This brought out the European, twice as brave as Lugard,[6] from the school-room where he had settled himself. He found Nyantechie on the ground nursing his ankle, crept back to the school and was shot at by the local escort constable who hadn't seen him go out and who fancied himself as something of a hunter.

Still, by the end of the week, the three wells were finished, with a concrete parapet and a rough awning of palm branches to keep out the dirt. There was a shallow depth of water in each, and as a parting gesture we all queued up, with the European and his clerk, to try it. It tasted terrible. But then, it was rare in our village for anyone to drink water except the children, and they complained that the water from the wells had no taste. The women liked it all right, although I suspect that, being women, what they liked most was the opportunity it gave them of arguing who should have the first use of the buckets.

One might have thought that that was the end of it, with no great harm done and everyone turning back again to a normal life. But the village was uneasy. We didn't like it and wondered what might come next. Then Opanin Kuntor fell sick, and swore beyond reason that it was the well water which had brought him down. He told his maidservant to fetch his water from the pool again, recovered quickly and went round the village triumphant, warning everyone of what they

[6] Frederick Lugard (1858–1945) was a British colonial administrator in Africa, especially in Nigeria.

might expect. Gradually, however, matters righted themselves. And we had something to take our minds off the Government in the 'outdooring' ceremony[7] of Kwame Tweneboa's child. This was a high occasion. Kwame was well over fifty, and although he had taken a second wife, neither had brought forth until now – and the woman herself was nearing forty. It called for a special celebration. We set to work, and Opanin Kuntor had the still going night and day in his yard. We had learned a lesson, too, from the previous occasion and decided to post sentries at the far edge of the village who would give the alarm should danger threaten: one shot for the local police, two for the Government Agent.

We slept well the night before the 'outdooring'. There wasn't a great deal to do on the farm so we ate and drank the day away, drank and gossiped into the night until the moon went down, when we went to bed and slept late. The next day, nearly the whole village went to pay their respects to the mother. The child, a boy, was named Osei Bonso after a famous ancestor of Kwame Tweneboa, and there was a good deal of friendly drinking, with the result that by mid-afternoon most of us were sleep again. The forenoon had been cloudy, with a leaden sky, driving us into the shelter of the neem trees which straddled the road, or to the shade of the compounds. Goats and sheep browsed in the bush, and a stray hen scratched lazily in the scrubby ditch by the school where you could see the children sprawled across their desks or asleep on the veranda.

Suddenly, there was the sound of a double shot; then, to our astonishment, two more. There was immediate confusion. The chief was still asleep; so were most of

[7] ceremony to mark the birth of a child and its naming

45

the elders. They were shaken into some kind of order while Opanin Kuntor hurried off to hide what was left of the *akpeteshie*. The rest of us collected round the chief's compound and held ourselves in reserve. There was the sound of a car, then another; the Government Agent pulled up outside the palace, and the driver signalled to a large touring car, which followed, to do the same. The Union Jack fluttered from the bonnet of the second car, and the driver – a uniformed constable – carefully chaperoned from the back seat an elderly European. Someone recognised him as the Regional Officer whom most of us knew to be next in power and glory to the Governor, if not to God Himself.

After the customary greetings had been made, with the Government Agent trotting up and down in attendance on the big man, we were told that the Regional Officer was interested in our town, that he had heard of our efforts to 'improve the amenities of the district through self-help', and had been good enough to interrupt a tour of inspection to visit us. This was said by the Government Agent in such solemn, satisfied tones that it was clear that, by digging the wells, we had helped more than ourselves.

Nana and the elders received this with perhaps less enthusiasm than they should have shown; they were alarmed at the second visit of the Government Agent, distrusted his intentions, and were concerned – as we all were – by the possible fate of the still and the rest of the drink. So it was with relief that we heard the Regional Officer saying that he would like to see the wells, and we led the way down the narrow path. Of course, when we got there, the Government Agent, with great satisfaction, thought he would like a drink. One of the women lowered the bucket into the nearest well and hauled it up on the rope. The Government Agent dipped a calabash into the half-bucket of water and handed it with delight to the Regional Officer who took a good mouthful, swallowed, then tried to spit it out, choking and spluttering with an agonised grimace. The Government Agent stared in amazement, and we looked uneasily at each other.

'Try it,' said the Regional Officer, and spat into the bush; 'try it yourself,' and he wiped his mouth with a folded handkerchief, still coughing and spitting, his eyes watering.

The Government Agent took a cautious sip, and a look of absolute disbelief came over his face. He turned, spat and shouted: 'Salifu, come here. Taste this.' The constable driver came forward and took a long draught. 'Fine.'

'What is it?'

'Gin, sir. Native gin.'

'How the devil did it get in there?' said the Regional Officer.

We all tried it then, including *Nana* who stood between the two Europeans. None of us said anything, however, for the few who guessed what had happened didn't care to tell. Eventually *Nana* spoke; and it says much for his presence of mind that he kept a serene countenance and a solemn note to his voice.

'Owura,' he said, addressing the Regional Officer, 'what has been done was necessary and right. The spirits are angry that we have left our forefathers' ways and the pool from which my father and his father's father drew their water. For this reason we have purified the well and placated the spirits with a little gin.'

'A little!' exclaimed the Regional Officer. 'What would it have tasted like if you had put in a lot?'

'*Akpeteshie?*' asked the Government Agent sharply.

'No, no,' said the chief, with a dignified air. 'That is

not allowed, although it would have been better and cheaper.'

The Government Agent looked at the Regional Officer, who said nothing. Then they turned and walked back to the village. I could see that the Regional Officer was amused; and slowly his good humour spread. By the time we reached the village there was a pleasant, unspoken accord between the two sides. Beer was fetched, and a bottle of whisky; the health of the Regional Officer, the Government Agent, the chief and elders, the village, and Kwame Tweneboa, were drunk. Finally, the two cars moved off and we went back to the palace.

'How much did you put in there?' asked the chief.

'*Nana*, it was three kerosene tins full,' said Opanin Kuntor. 'I was afraid. But I put the tins in complete. They must have leaked.'

'Ah,' said the chief. 'I'm sure they did.'

The Answer Is No

by Naguib Mahfouz

The important piece of news that the new headmaster had arrived spread through the school. She heard of it in the women teachers' common room as she was casting a final glance at the day's lessons. There was no getting away from joining the other teachers in congratulating him, and from shaking him by the hand too. A shudder passed through her body, but it was unavoidable.

'They speak highly of his ability,' said a colleague of hers. 'And they talk too of his strictness.'

It had always been a possibility that might occur, and now it had. Her pretty face paled, and a staring look came to her wide black eyes.

When the time came, the teachers went in single file, decorously attired, to his open room. He stood behind his desk as he received the men and women. He was of medium height, with a tendency to portliness, and had a spherical face, hooked nose, and bulging eyes; the first thing that could be seen of him was a thick, puffed-up moustache, arched like a foam-laden wave. She advanced with her eyes fixed on his chest. Avoiding his gaze, she stretched out her hand. What was she to say? Just what the others had said? However, she kept silent, uttered not a word. What, she wondered, did his eyes express? His rough hand shook hers, and he said in a gruff voice, 'Thanks.' She turned elegantly and moved off.

She forgot her worries through her daily tasks,

though she did not look in good shape. Several of the girls remarked, 'Miss is in a bad mood.' When she returned to her home at the beginning of the Pyramids Road, she changed her clothes and sat down to eat with her mother. 'Everything all right?' enquired her mother, looking her in the face.

'Badran, Badran Badawi,' she said briefly. 'Do you remember him? He's been appointed our headmaster.'

'Really!'

Then, after a moment of silence, she said, 'It's of no importance at all – it's an old and long-forgotten story.'

After eating, she took herself off to her study to rest for a while before correcting some exercise books. She had forgotten him completely. No, not completely. How could he be forgotten completely? When he had first come to give her a private lesson in mathematics, she was fourteen years of age. In fact not quite fourteen. He had been twenty-five years older, the same age as her father. She had said to her mother, 'His appearance is a mess, but he explains things well.' And her mother had said, 'We're not concerned with what he looks like; what's important is how he explains things.'

He was an amusing person, and she got on well with him and benefited from his knowledge. How, then, had it happened? In her innocence she had not noticed any change in his behaviour to put her on her guard. Then one day he had been left on his own with her, her father having gone to her aunt's clinic. She had not the slightest doubts about a man she regarded as a second father. How, then, had it happened? Without love or desire on her part the thing had happened. She had asked in terror about what had occurred, and he had told her, 'Don't be frightened or sad. Keep it to yourself and I'll come and propose to you the day you come of age.'

And he had kept his promise and had come to ask for

her hand. By then she had attained a degree of maturity that gave her an understanding of the dimensions of her tragic position. She had found that she had no love or respect for him and that he was as far as he could be from her dreams and from the ideas she had formed of what constituted an ideal and moral person. But what was to be done? Her father had passed away two years ago, and her mother had been taken aback by the forwardness of the man. However, she had said to her, 'I know your attachment to your personal independence, so I leave the decision to you.'

She had been conscious of the critical position she was in. She had either to accept or to close the door for ever. It was the sort of situation that could force her into something she detested. She was the rich, beautiful girl, a byword in Abbasiyya for her nobility of character, and now here she was struggling helplessly in a well-sprung trap, while he looked down at her with rapacious eyes. Just as she had hated his strength, so too did she hate her own weakness. To have abused her innocence was one thing, but for him to have the upper hand now that she was fully in possession of her faculties was something else. He had said, 'So here I am, making good my promise because I love you.' He had also said, 'I know of your love of teaching, and you will complete your studies at the College of Science.'

She had felt such anger as she had never felt before. She had rejected coercion in the same way as she rejected ugliness. It had meant little to her to sacrifice marriage. She had welcomed being on her own, for solitude accompanied by self-respect was not loneliness. She had also guessed he was after her money. She had told her mother quite straightforwardly, 'No,' to which her mother had replied, 'I am astonished you did not make this decision from the first moment.'

The man had blocked her way outside and said, 'How can you refuse? Don't you realise the outcome?' And she had replied with an asperity he had not expected, 'For me any outcome is preferable to being married to you.'

After finishing her studies, she had wanted something to do to fill her spare time, so she had worked as a teacher. Chances to marry had come time after time, but she had turned her back on them all.

'Does no one please you?' her mother asked her.

'I know what I'm doing,' she had said gently.

'But time is going by.'

'Let it go as it pleases, I am content.'

Day by day she becomes older. She avoids love, fears it. With all her strength she hopes that life will pass calmly, peacefully, rather than happily. She goes on persuading herself that happiness is not confined to love and motherhood. Never has she regretted her firm decision. Who knows what the morrow holds? But she was certainly unhappy that he should again make his appearance in her life, that she would be dealing with him day after day, and that he would be making of the past a living and painful present.

Then, the first time he was alone with her in his room, he asked her, 'How are you?'

She answered coldly, 'I'm fine.'

He hesitated slightly before enquiring, 'Have you not ... I mean, did you get married?'

In the tone of someone intent on cutting short a conversation, she said, 'I told you, I'm fine.'

Another Evening at the Club

by Alifa Rifaat

In a state of tension, she awaited the return of her husband. At a loss to predict what would happen between them, she moved herself back and forth in the rocking chair on the wide wooden verandah that ran along the bank and occupied part of the river itself, its supports being fixed in the river bed, while around it grew grasses and reeds. As though to banish her apprehension, she passed her fingers across her hair. The spectres of the eucalyptus trees ranged along the garden fence rocked before her gaze, with white egrets slumbering on their high branches like huge white flowers among the thin leaves.

The crescent moon rose from behind the eastern mountains and the peaks of the gently stirring waves glistened in its feeble rays, intermingled with threads of light leaking from the houses of Manfaicut scattered along the opposite bank. The coloured bulbs fixed to the trees in the garden of the club at the far end of the town stood out against the surrounding darkness. Somewhere over there her husband now sat, most likely engrossed in a game of chess.

It was only a few years ago that she had first laid eyes on him at her father's house, meeting his gaze that weighed up her beauty and priced it before offering the dowry. She had noted his eyes ranging over her as she presented him with the coffee in the Japanese cups that were kept safely locked away in the cupboard for important guests. Her mother had herself laid them out on the silver-plated tray with its elaborately embroidered spread. When the two men had taken their coffee, her father had looked up at her with a smile and had told her to sit down, and she had seated herself on the sofa facing them, drawing the end of her dress over her knees and looking through lowered lids at the man who might choose her as his wife. She had been glad to see that he was tall, well-built and clean-shaven except for a thin greying moustache. In particular she noticed the well-cut coat of English tweed and the silk shirt with gold links. She had felt herself blushing as she saw him returning her gaze. Then the man turned to her father and took out a gold case and offered him a cigarette.

'You really shouldn't, my dear sir,' said her father, patting his chest with his left hand and extracting a cigarette with trembling fingers. Before he could bring out his box of matches, Abboud-Bey had produced his lighter.

'No, after you, my dear sir,' said her father in embarrassment. Mingled with her sense of excitement at this man who gave out such an air of worldly self-confidence was a guilty shame at her father's inadequacy.

After lighting her father's cigarette, Abboud-Bey sat back, crossing his legs, and took out a cigarette for himself. He tapped it against the case before putting it in the corner of his mouth and lighting it; then he blew out circles of smoke that followed each other across the room.

'It's a great honour for us, my son,' said her father, smiling first at Abboud-Bey, then at his daughter, at which Abboud-Bey looked across at her and asked:

'And the beautiful little girl's still at secondary school?'

She had lowered her head modestly and her father had answered:

'And from today she'll be staying at home in readiness for your happy life together, Allah permitting,' and at a glance from her father she had hurried off to join her mother in the kitchen.

'You're a lucky girl,' her mother had told her. 'He's a real find. Any girl would be happy to have him. He's an Inspector of Irrigation, though he's not yet forty. He earns a big salary and gets a fully furnished government house wherever he's posted, which will save us the expense of setting up a house – and I don't have to tell you what our situation is – and that's besides the house he owns in Alexandria where you'll be spending your holidays.'

Samia had wondered to herself how such a splendid suitor had found his way to her door. Who had told him that Mr Mahmoud Barakat, a mere clerk at the Court of Appeal, had a beautiful daughter of good reputation?

The days were then taken up with going the rounds of Cairo's shops and choosing clothes for the new grand life she would be living. This was made possible by her father borrowing on the security of his government pension. Abboud-Bey, on his part, never visited her without bringing a present. For her birthday, just before they were married, he bought her an emerald ring that came in a plush box bearing the name of a well-known jeweller in Kasr el-Nil Street. On her wedding night, as he put a diamond bracelet round her wrist, he had reminded her that she was marrying someone with a brilliant career in front of him and that one of the most important things in life was the opinions of others, particularly one's equals and seniors. Though she was still only a young girl she must try to act with suitable dignity.

'Tell people you're from the well-known Barakat family and that your father was a judge,' and he went up to her and gently patted her cheeks in a fatherly, reassuring gesture that he was often to repeat during their times together.

Then, yesterday evening, she had returned from the club somewhat lightheaded from the bottle of beer she had been required to drink on the occasion of someone's birthday. Her husband, noting the state she was in, hurriedly took her back home. She had undressed and put on her night-gown, leaving her jewellery on the dressing table, and was fast asleep seconds after getting into bed. The following morning, fully recovered, she slept late, then rang the bell as usual and had breakfast brought to her. It was only as she was putting her jewellery away in the wooden and mother-of-pearl box that she realised her emerald ring was missing.

Could it have dropped from her finger at the club, in the car on the way back? No, she distinctly remembered it last thing at night, remembered the usual difficulty she had in getting it off her finger. She stripped the bed of its sheets, turned over the mattress, looked inside the pillow cases, crawled on hands and knees under the bed. The tray of breakfast lying on the small bedside table caught her eye and she remembered the young servant coming in that morning with it, remembered the noise of the tray being put down, the curtains being drawn, the tray then being lifted up again and placed on the bedside table. No one but the servant had entered the room. Should she call her and question her?

Eventually, having taken two aspirins, she decided to do nothing and await the return of her husband from work.

Directly he arrived, she told him what had happened and he took her by the arm and seated her down beside him:

'Let's just calm down and go over what happened.'

She repeated, this time with further details, the whole story.

'And you've looked for it?'

'Everywhere. Every possible and impossible place in the bedroom and the bathroom. You see, I remember distinctly taking if off last night.'

He grimaced at the thought of last night, then said:

'Anybody been in the room since Gazia when she brought in the breakfast?'

'Not a soul. I've even told Gazia not to do the room today.'

'And you've not mentioned anything to her?'

'I thought I'd better leave it to you.'

'Fine, go and tell her I want to speak to her. There's no point in your saying anything, but I think it would be as well if you were present when I talk to her.'

Five minutes later Gazia, the young servant girl they had recently employed, entered behind her mistress. Samia took herself to a far corner of the room while Gazia stood in front of Abboud-Bey, her hands folded across her chest, her eyes lowered.

'Yes, sir?'

'Where's the ring?'

'What ring are you talking about, sir?'

'Now don't make out you don't know. The one with the green stone. It would be better for you if you hand it over and then nothing more need be said.'

'May Allah blind me if I've set eyes on it.'

He stood up and gave her a sudden slap on the face. The girl reeled back, put one hand to her cheek, then lowered it again to her chest and made no answer to any of Abboud's questions. Finally he said to her:

'You've got just fifteen seconds to say where you've

hidden the ring or else, I swear to you, you're not going to have a good time of it.'

As he lifted up his arm to look at his watch the girl flinched slightly but continued in her silence. When he went to the telephone, Samia raised her head and saw that the girl's cheeks were wet with tears. Abboud-Bey got through to the Superintendent of police and told him briefly what had occurred.

'Of course I haven't got any actual proof but seeing that no one else entered the room, it's obvious she's pinched it. Anyway I'll leave the matter in your capable hands. I know your people have their ways and means.' He gave a short laugh, then listened for a while and said: 'I'm really most grateful to you.' He put down the receiver and turned round to Samia:

'That's it, my dear. There's nothing more to worry about. The Superintendent has promised me we'll certainly get it back. The patrol car's on the way.'

The following day, in the late afternoon, she'd been sitting in front of her dressing table rearranging her jewellery in its box when an earring slipped from her grasp and fell to the floor. As she bent to pick it up she saw the emerald ring stuck between the leg of the table and the wall. Since that moment she had sat in a state of panic awaiting her husband's return from the club. She even felt tempted to walk down to the water's edge and throw it into the river so as to be rid of the unpleasantness that lay ahead.

At the sound of the screech of tyres rounding the house to the garage, she slipped the ring on to her finger. As he entered she stood up and raised her hand to show him the ring. Quickly, trying to choose her words but knowing that she was expressing herself clumsily, she explained what an extraordinary thing it was that it should have lodged itself between the dressing table and the wall, what an extraordinary coincidence she would have dropped the earring and so seen it, how she'd thought of ringing him at the club to tell him the good news but ...

She stopped in mid-sentence when she saw his frown and added weakly:

'I'm sorry. I can't think how it could have happened. What do we do now?'

He shrugged his shoulders as though in surprise.

'Are you asking me, my dear lady? Nothing of course.'

'But they've been beating up the girl – you yourself said they'd not let her be till she confessed.'

Unhurriedly, he sat himself down as though to consider this new aspect of the matter. Taking out his case, he tapped a cigarette against it in his accustomed manner, then moistened his lips, put the cigarette in place and lit it. The smoke rings hovered in the still air as he looked at his watch and said:

'In any case she's not got all that long before they let her go. They can't keep her for more than forty-eight hours without getting any evidence or a confession. It won't kill her to put up with things for a while longer. By now the whole town knows the servant stole the ring – or would you like me to tell everyone: "Look, folks, the fact is that the wife got a bit tiddly on a couple of sips of beer and the ring took off on its own and hid itself behind the dressing table? What do you think?"'

'I know the situation's a bit awkward ...'

'Awkward? It's downright ludicrous. Listen, there's nothing to be done but to give it to me and the next time I go down to Cairo I'll sell it and get something else in its place. We'd be the laughing-stock of the town.'

He stretched out his hand and she found herself taking off the ring and placing it in the outstretched palm. She was careful that their eyes should not meet. For a moment she was on the point of protesting and in fact uttered a few words:

'I'd just like to say we could . . .'

Putting the ring away in his pocket, he bent over her and with both hands gently patted her on the cheeks. It was a gesture she had long become used to, a gesture that promised her continued security, that told her that this man who was her husband and the father of her child had also taken the place of her father who, as though assured that he had found her a suitable substitute, had followed up her marriage with his own funeral. The gesture told her more eloquently than any words that he was the man, she the woman, he the one who carried the responsibilities, made the decisions; she the one whose role it was to be beautiful, happy, carefree. Now, though, for the first time in their life together, the gesture came like a slap in the face.

Directly he removed his hands her whole body was seized with an uncontrollable trembling. Frightened he would notice, she rose to her feet and walked with deliberate steps towards the large window. She leaned her forehead against the comforting cold surface and closed her eyes tightly for several seconds. When she opened them, she noticed that the café lights strung between the trees on the opposite shore had been turned on and that there were men seated under them and a waiter moving among the tables. The dark shape of a boat momentarily blocked out the café scene; in the light from the hurricane lamp hanging from its bow she saw it cutting through several of those floating islands of Nile waterlilies that, rootless, are swept along with the current.

Suddenly she became aware of his presence along-side her.

'Why don't you go and change quickly while I take the car out? It's hot and it would be nice to have supper at the club.'

'As you like. Why not?'

By the time she had turned round from the window, she was smiling.

The Story of the Chest

by Marguerite Amrouche

May my story be beautiful and unwind like a long thread ...

Once there was a king – though there is no other king but God – and this king had a dearly beloved son who said to him, 'King, my father, let me go to the market and see your subjects.'

'Do what you please,' the king replied to him.

So the prince went to market, and he said to all the men there, 'You must not sell nor buy, you must not buy nor sell, until you can answer these riddles. Who is it who, in the morning, walks on four feet, at noon, on two, and on three in the evening? Second, what tree has twelve branches with thirty leaves to a branch?' No one knew what to answer. All were mute. The marketers dispersed. A week went by. The next market day brought back the king's son. He asked, 'Have you found the answers to my riddles?'

Once again, all were silent, and they went away. He who went to buy, bought not. And he who went to sell, sold not. The market closed. But, among those assembled was the market supervisor. He was very poor and had two daughters – one very beautiful and the other, the younger, slight but keen of mind. In the evening when her father came home, the younger said to him,

'Father, for two market days you left home, but you returned empty-handed. Why?'

'My daughter,' he replied, 'the king's son came and told us not to buy or sell, and not to sell or buy until we would know the meaning of what he was going to say.'

'And what did the prince ask you to guess?' replied the girl.

'He asked us: "Who is it who in the morning walks on four feet, at noon, on two, and on three in the evening? And, what tree has twelve branches with thirty leaves to a branch?"'

His daughter reflected a little before replying: 'It's easy, father, He who walks in the morning on four feet, at noon, on two, and on three in the evening is Man. In the morning of his life, he crawls on all fours, later, he goes on two feet, and when he is old he leans on a cane. As for the tree, it is the year; the year has twelve months and each month has thirty days.'

A week went by – in its course it brought another market day and with it the king's son. He asked, 'And today have you figured it out?'

The supervisor spoke up. He said, 'Yes, my lord. He who walks in the morning on four feet, on two at noon, and on three in the evening is Man. In the morning of his life, he crawls on all fours, older he goes on two feet, and when he is old he leans on a cane. As for the tree, it is the year; the year has twelve months and each month has thirty days.'

'Open up the market!' commanded the king's son. Then evening fell; the prince approached the supervisor and said to him, 'I want to go to your house.' The supervisor replied, 'Good, sir.' And they went off together on foot. The prince declared, 'I have fled from God's paradise. I refused what God desired. The way is long; carry me or I shall carry you. Speak, or I shall speak.' The supervisor kept still. They came to a river and the king's son said, 'Make me cross the river or I

shall make you cross it.' The supervisor, who understood nothing of this, did not answer. They arrived at
the house.

The younger daughter of the supervisor (she who
was frail but intuitive), opened the door for them and
said, 'Welcome. My mother has gone out to see
someone she has never seen. My brothers are fighting
water with water. My sister finds herself between two
walls.'

The king's son came in. Looking at the most
beautiful daughter, he said, 'The plate is beautiful, but
it has a crack in it.'

Night found the whole family united. One had killed
a chicken and one had prepared a holiday couscous.
When the meal was ready, the prince said, 'Let me be
the one to serve the chicken.' He gave the head to the
father, the wings to the daughters, the thighs to the two
sons, the breast to the mother. He kept the feet for
himself. Everyone ate and then got ready to spend the
evening. The king's son turned toward the lively
daughter and told her, 'In order for you to tell me "My
mother has gone to see someone she has never seen"
she would have to be a midwife. For you to say to me
"My brothers are fighting water with water," they must
have been watering the gardens. As for your sister
"between two walls" she would be weaving with a wall
behind her and a wall before her – the nature of the
trade.'

The girl replied, 'When you started out, you told my
father "I have fled from God's paradise". That's the
rain, which makes a paradise on earth – so you were
afraid of getting wet. And when you said, "I refused
what God desired" – was it death you were refusing?
God wants us all to die, but we don't want to. Finally you
said to my father "The way is long, carry me or I shall

carry you. Speak or I shall speak" so that the journey would seem shorter. Just as you told him, when you found yourselves beside the river "Make me cross the river or I shall make you cross it" you meant, "show me the ford or I shall seek it." When you entered our house, you looked at my sister and said, "The plate is beautiful, but it has a crack in it." My sister is truly beautiful and virtuous too, but she is the daughter of a poor man. And then you divided the chicken. You gave the head to my father because he is the head of the household. You gave the breast to my mother for she is the heart of the house. To us, the girls, you gave the wings, because we won't stay home here; we'll take flight. You gave my brothers the thighs; they will be the support, the pillars of the house. And for yourself you took the claws because you are the guest; your feet brought you here and your feet will take you away.'

On the next day the prince went to find the king, his father, and said to him, 'I wish to marry the market supervisor's daughter.'

The king exclaimed indignantly, 'How could you, the son of a king, marry the daughter of a supervisor? It would be shameful. We would become the laughing stock of our neighbours.'

'If I don't marry her,' said the prince, 'I shall never marry at all.'

The king, who had no other son, ended by conceding: 'Marry her, then, my son, since you do love her.'

The prince offered his fiancée gold and silver, silks and satins, and all kinds of marvels. But he also said to her gravely, 'Remember this well. The day your wisdom surpasses my own, that day will we part.'

She answered, 'I will always do everything that you

wish.' Nonetheless, before the wedding day, she sent for the carpenter and ordered a chest made the size for a man, with a cover to be pierced with small holes. For the chest she wove a satin lining. She put her trousseau in it and sent it to the home of her bridegroom.

The nuptials were followed by rejoicing which lasted seven days and seven nights. The king served a great feast. For many years after, the prince and princess lived happily at the court. And when the king died, his son succeeded him.

One day when the young king was dispensing justice, two women came before him with a child they were quarrelling over. One said, 'He's my son!' and the other claimed, 'He's mine.' They got to shouting and tearing each other's hair. The king was perplexed. The queen, curious, found out about it from a servant, who told her, 'Two women are there with a child whom both are claiming. Each one had a baby, but one of the babies died. And the king hasn't been able to find out which is the mother of the living child.' The queen thought it over for a moment. Then she replied, 'Let the king simply say to the two women, "I shall divide the child in two, and each of you may have half." Then he will hear the true mother cry out, "Lord, don't kill him, in God's name!"'

The servant ran to tell the king the trick which would bring out the truth. The king turned toward his minister, saying, 'Bring forth a blade so we can divide this child.' 'No, Lord' cried out one of the women, 'He will die!' So the king held out the child to her and said, 'You are the mother for you did not want him to die.'

Then the king went off to find the queen. He told her, 'Do you remember what we agreed to on our wedding day? I said to you, "The day your wisdom surpasses my own, that day will we part."'

She answered, 'I do remember. But grant me just one favour. Let us eat together for the last time. Then I shall leave.'

He consented, and added, 'Choose whatever you wish in the palace and take it with you.'

She herself prepared the meal. She gave the king a drug without his suspecting it. He ate, he drank, and suddenly he fell asleep. She lifted him up and put him in the chest, and then carefully closed the lid over him. She called the servants and informed them that she was going to the country for a family visit. She directed them to move the chest cautiously. And she left the palace, never losing sight of the chest which followed.

Once she was back in her parents' home, she opened the chest. She took her husband tenderly in her arms and stretched him out on the bed. Seated at the head of the bed, she waited patiently for him to wake up. It was evening before the king opened his eyes, saying, 'Where am I? And who brought me here?'

She answered, 'I did.'

Then he spoke again to her, 'Why? How did I get here?'

And she answered him, smiling, 'Remember when you told me, "Look around you, and take whatever pleases you in the palace and bring it with you"? Nothing else in the palace could be as dear to me as you. So I took *you*. And I brought you here in a chest.' Now they understood one another. They returned to the palace and lived happily there together until they died.

My story runs on like a brook; I have told it to the lords.

No Witchcraft for Sale

by Doris Lessing

The Farquars had been childless for years when little
Teddy was born; and they were touched by the pleasure
of their servants, who brought presents of fowls and
eggs and flowers to the homestead when they came to
rejoice over the baby, exclaiming with delight over his
downy golden head and his blue eyes. They congratu-
lated Mrs Farquar as if she had achieved a very great
thing, and she felt that she had – her smile for the
lingering, admiring natives was warm and grateful.

Later, when Teddy had his first haircut, Gideon the
cook picked up the soft gold tufts from the ground, and
held them reverently in his hand. Then he smiled at the
little boy and said: 'Little Yellow Head.' That became
the native name for the child. Gideon and Teddy were
great friends from the first. When Gideon had finished
his work, he would lift Teddy on his shoulders to the
shade of a big tree, and play with him there, forming
curious little toys from twigs and leaves and grass, or
shaping animals from wetted soil. When Teddy learned
to walk it was often Gideon who crouched before him,
clucking encouragement, finally catching him when he
fell, tossing him up in the air till they both became
breathless with laughter. Mrs Farquar was fond of the
old cook because of his love for her child.

There was no second baby; and one day Gideon said:
'Ah missus, missus, the Lord above sent this one; Little
Yellow Head is the most good thing we have in our

house.' Because of that 'we' Mrs Farquar felt a warm impulse towards her cook; and at the end of the month she raised his wages. He had been with her now for several years; he was one of the few natives who had his wife and children in the compound and never wanted to go home to his kraal,[1] which was some hundreds of miles away. Sometimes a small piccanin who had been born the same time as Teddy, could be seen peering from the edge of the bush, staring in awe at the little white boy with his miraculous fair hair and northern blue eyes. The two little children would gaze at each other with a wide, interested gaze, and once Teddy put out his hand curiously to touch the black child's cheeks and hair.

Gideon, who was watching, shook his head wonderingly, and said: 'Ah, missus, these are both children, and one will grow up to be a Baas,[2] and one will be a servant'; and Mrs Farquar smiled and said sadly, 'Yes, Gideon, I was thinking the same.' She sighed. 'It is God's will,' said Gideon, who was mission boy. The Farquars were very religious people; and this shared feeling about God bound servant and masters even closer together.

Teddy was about six years old when he was given a scooter, and discovered the intoxications of speed. All day he would fly around the homestead, in and out of flowerbeds, scattering squawking chickens and irritated dogs, finishing with a wide dizzying arc into the kitchen door. There he would cry: 'Gideon, look at me!' And Gideon would laugh and say: 'Very clever, Little Yellow Head.' Gideon's youngest son, who was now a herdsboy, came especially up from the compound to see the scooter. He was afraid to come near it, but Teddy

[1] village of huts clustered together
[2] Boss

showed off in front of him. 'Piccanin,' shouted Teddy, 'get out of my way!' And he raced in circles around the black child until he was frightened, and fled back to the bush.

'Why did you frighten him?' asked Gideon, gravely reproachful.

Teddy said defiantly: 'He's only a black boy,' and laughed. Then, when Gideon turned away from him without speaking, his face fell. Very soon he slipped into the house and found an orange and brought it to Gideon, saying: 'This is for you.' He could not bring himself to say he was sorry; but he could not bear to lose Gideon's affection either. Gideon took the orange unwillingly and sighed. 'Soon you will be going away to school, Little Yellow Head,' he said wonderingly, 'and then you will be grown up.' He shook his head gently and said, 'And that is how our lives go.' He seemed to be putting a distance between himself and Teddy, not because of resentment, but in the way a person accepts something inevitable. The baby had lain in his arms and smiled up into his face: the tiny boy had swung from his shoulders had played with him by the hour. Now Gideon would not let his flesh touch the flesh of the white child. He was kind, but there was a grave formality in his voice that made Teddy pout and sulk away. Also, it made him into a man: with Gideon he was polite, and carried himself formally, and if he came into the kitchen to ask for something, it was in the way a white man uses towards a servant, expecting to be obeyed.

But on the day that Teddy came staggering into the kitchen with his fists to his eyes, shrieking with pain, Gideon dropped the pot full of hot soup that he was holding, rushed to the child, and forced aside his fingers. 'A snake!' he exclaimed. Teddy had been on his scooter, and had come to a rest with his foot on the side of a big tub of plants. A tree-snake, hanging by its tail from the roof, had spat full into his eyes. Mrs Farquar came running when she heard the commotion. 'He'll go blind,' she sobbed, holding Teddy close against her. 'Gideon, he'll go blind!' Already the eyes, with perhaps half an hour's sight left in them, were swollen up to the size of fists: Teddy's small white face was distorted by great purple oozing protuberances. Gideon said: 'Wait a minute, missus, I'll get some medicine.' He ran off into the bush.

Mrs Farquar lifted the child into the house and bathed his eyes with permanganate. She had scarcely heard Gideon's words; but when she saw that her remedies had no effect at all, and remembered how she had seen natives with no sight in their eyes, because of the spitting of a snake, she began to look for the return of her cook, remembering what she had heard of the efficacy of native herbs. She stood by the window, holding the terrified, sobbing little boy in her arms, and peered helplessly into the bush. It was not more than a few minutes before she saw Gideon come bounding back, and in his hand he held a plant.

'Do not be afraid, missus,' said Gideon, 'this will cure Little Yellow Head's eyes.' He stripped the leaves from the plant, leaving a small white fleshy root. Without even washing it, he put the root in his mouth, chewed it vigorously, and then held the spittle there while he took the child forcibly from Mrs Farquar. He gripped Teddy down between his knees, and pressed the balls of his thumbs into the swollen eyes, so that the child screamed and Mrs Farquar cried out in protest: 'Gideon, Gideon!' But Gideon took no notice. He knelt over the writhing child, pushing back the puffy lids till chinks of eyeball showed, and then he spat hard, again and again, into first one eye, and then the other. He finally lifted Teddy gently into his mother's arms, and said: 'His eyes will get better.' But Mrs Farquar was weeping with terror, and she could hardly thank him: it was impossible to believe that Teddy could keep his sight. In a couple of hours the swellings were gone; the eyes were inflamed and tender but Teddy could see. Mr and Mrs Farquar went to Gideon in the kitchen and thanked him over and over again. They felt helpless because of their gratitude: it seemed they could do nothing to express it. They gave Gideon presents for his wife and children, and a big increase in wages, but these things could not pay for Teddy's now completely cured eyes. Mrs Farquar said: 'Gideon, God chose you as an instrument for His goodness,' and Gideon said: 'Yes, missus, God is very good.'

Now, when such a thing happens on a farm, it cannot be long before everyone hears of it. Mr and Mrs Farquar told their neighbours and the story was discussed from one end of the district to the other. The bush is full of secrets. No one can live in Africa, or at least on the veld,[3] without learning very soon that there is an ancient wisdom of leaf and soil and season – and, too, perhaps most important of all, of the darker tracts of the human mind – which is the black man's heritage. Up and down the district people were telling anecdotes, reminding each other of things that had happened to them.

'But I saw it myself, I tell you. It was a puff-adder bite. The kaffir's[4] arm was swollen to the elbow, like a great shiny black bladder. He was groggy after half a minute. He was dying. Then suddenly a kaffir walked out of the

[3] open or thinly forested grass country
[4] a member of the Bantu community in South Africa and an offensive term for a black South African

bush with his hands full of green stuff. He 、
something on the place, and next day my boy was
at work, and all you could see was two small punctu.
in the skin.'

This was the kind of tale they told. And, as always,
with a certain amount of exasperation, because while
all of them knew that in the bush of Africa are waiting
valuable drugs locked in bark, in simple-looking leaves,
in roots, it was impossible to ever get the truth about
them from the natives themselves.

The story eventually reached town; and perhaps it
was at a sundowner party, or some such function, that a
doctor, who happened to be there, challenged it.
'Nonsense,' he said. 'These things get exaggerated in
the telling. We are always checking up on this kind of
story, and we draw a blank every time.'

Anyway, one morning there arrived a strange car at
the homestead, and out stepped one of the workers
from the laboratory in town, with cases full of test-tubes
and chemicals.

Mr and Mrs Farquar were flustered and pleased and
flattered. They asked the scientist to lunch, and they
told the story all over again, for the hundredth time.
Little Teddy was there too, his blue eyes sparkling with
health, to prove the truth of it. The scientist explained
how humanity might benefit if this new drug could be
offered for sale; and the Farquars were even more
pleased: they were kind, simple people, who liked to
think of something good coming about because of
them. But when the scientist began talking of the
money that might result, their manner showed discomfort. Their feelings over the miracle (that was how they
thought of it) were so strong and deep and religious,
that it was distasteful to them to think of money. The
scientist, seeing their faces, went back to his first point,

73

advancement of humanity. He was
perfunctory: it was not the first time he
the tail of a fabulous bush-secret.

hen the meal was over, the Farquars
nto their living-room and explained to
as, here, was a Big Doctor from the Big
City, and he had come all that way to see Gideon. At this
Gideon seemed afraid; he did not understand; and
Mrs Farquar explained quickly that it was because of
the wonderful thing he had done with Teddy's eyes that
the Big Baas had come.

Gideon looked from Mrs Farquar to Mr Farquar, and
then at the little boy, who was showing great importance because of the occasion. At last he said grudgingly: 'The Big Baas wants to know what medicine I
used?' He spoke incredulously, as if he could not
believe his old friends could so betray him. Mr Farquar
began explaining how a useful medicine could be made
out of the root, and how it could be put on sale, and
how thousands of people, black and white, up and down
the continent of Africa, could be saved by the medicine
when that spitting snake filled their eyes with poison.
Gideon listened, his eyes bent on the ground, the skin
of his forehead puckering in discomfort. When
Mr Farquar had finished he did not reply. The scientist,
who all this time had been leaning back in a big chair,
sipping his coffee and smiling with sceptical good-
humour, chipped in and explained all over again, in
different words, about the making of drugs and the
progress of science. Also, he offered Gideon a present.

There was silence after this further explanation, and
then Gideon remarked indifferently that he could not
remember the root. His face was sullen and hostile,
even when he looked at the Farquars, whom he usually
treated like old friends. They were beginning to feel

74

annoyed; and this feeling annulled the guilt that had been sprung into life by Gideon's accusing manner. They were beginning to feel that he was unreasonable. But it was at that moment that they all realised he would never give in. The magical drug would remain where it was, unknown and useless except for the tiny scattering of Africans who had the knowledge, natives who might be digging a ditch for the municipality in a ragged shirt and a pair of patched shorts, but who were still born to healing, hereditary healers, being the nephews or sons of the old witch doctors whose ugly masks and bits of bone and all the uncouth properties of magic were the outward signs of real power and wisdom.

The Farquars might tread on that plant fifty times a day as they passed from house to garden, from cow kraal to mealie field, but they would never know it.

But they went on persuading and arguing, with all the force of their exasperation; and Gideon continued to say that he could not remember, or that there was no such root, or that it was the wrong season of the year, or that it wasn't the root itself, but the spit from his mouth that had cured Teddy's eyes. He said all these things one after another, and seemed not to care they were contradictory. He was rude and stubborn. The Farquars could hardly recognise their gentle, lovable old servant in this ignorant, perversely obstinate African, standing there in front of them with lowered eyes, his hands twitching his cook's apron, repeating over and over whichever one of the stupid refusals that first entered his head.

And suddenly he appeared to give in. He lifted his head, gave a long, blank angry look at the circle of whites, who seemed to him like a circle of yelping dogs pressing around him, and said: 'I will show you the root.'

They walked single file away from the homestead down a kaffir path. It was a blazing December afternoon, with the sky full of hot rain-clouds. Everything was hot: the sun was like a bronze tray whirling overhead, there was a heat shimmer over the fields, the soil was scorching underfoot, the dusty wind blew gritty and thick and warm in their faces. It was a terrible day, fit only for reclining on a verandah with iced drinks, which is where they would normally have been at that hour.

From time to time, remembering that on the day of the snake it had taken ten minutes to find the root, someone asked: 'Is it much further, Gideon?' And Gideon would answer over his shoulder, with angry politeness: 'I'm looking for the root, baas.' And indeed, he would frequently bend sideways and trail his hand among the grasses with a gesture that was insulting in its perfunctoriness. He walked them through the bush along unknown paths for two hours, in that melting destroying heat, so that the sweat trickled coldly down them and their heads ached. They were all quite silent: the Farquars because they were angry, the scientist because he was being proved right again; there was no such plant. His was a tactful silence.

At last, six miles from the house, Gideon suddenly decided they had had enough; or perhaps his anger evaporated at that moment. He picked up, without an attempt at looking anything but casual, a handful of blue flowers from the grass, flowers that had been growing plentifully all down the paths they had come.

He handed them to the scientist without looking at him, and marched off by himself on the way home, leaving them to follow him if they chose.

When they got back to the house, the scientist went to the kitchen to thank Gideon: he was being very polite, even though there was an amused look in his eyes. Gideon was not there. Throwing the flowers casually into the back of his car, the eminent visitor departed on his way back to his laboratory.

Gideon was back in his kitchen in time to prepare dinner, but he was sulking. He spoke to Mrs Farquar like an unwilling servant. It was days before they liked each other again.

The Farquars made enquiries about the root from their labourers. Sometimes they were answered with distrustful stares. Sometimes the natives said: 'We do not know. We have never heard of the root.' One, the cattle boy, who had been with them a long time, and had grown to trust them a little said: 'Ask your boy in the kitchen. Now, there's a doctor for you. He's the son of a famous medicine man who used to be in these parts, and there's nothing he cannot cure.' Then he added politely: 'Of course, he's not as good as the whiteman's doctor, we know that, but he's good for us.'

After some time, when the soreness had gone from between the Farquars and Gideon, they began to joke: 'When are you going to show us the snake-root, Gideon?' And he would laugh and shake his head, saying, a little uncomfortably: 'But I did show you, missus, have you forgotten?'

Much later, Teddy, as a schoolboy, would come into the kitchen and say: 'You old rascal, Gideon! Do you remember that time you tricked us all by making us walk miles all over the veld for nothing? It was so far my father had to carry me!'

And Gideon would double up with polite laughter. After much laughing, he would suddenly straighten himself up, wipe his old eyes, and look sadly at Teddy, who was grinning mischievously at him across the kitchen: 'Ah, Little Yellow Head, how you have grown! Soon you will be grown up with a farm of your own ...'

The Advance

by Henry Lopes

'No good,' the little girl said, screwing up her face.

'Yes it is, Françoise. Look.' Carmen herself swallowed a mandarin section, then closed her eyes. The little girl looked at her, impassively.

'Eat it all up.'

Like a priest proffering the host, Carmen offered her the orange quarter. Haughtily, the little girl turned her head away. It was already seven o'clock. Carmen was eager to finish up her work, especially since she had not yet asked the mistress ...

She spoke more sharply and looked stern.

'If you don't eat, Françoise, I'm going to tell your mother.' Still the little girl did not relent.

The mistress of the house was in the living-room, together with her husband, entertaining friends they had invited over for bridge. She had already warned Carmen several times not to bother her when she was, as she said, 'with company'. Did Carmen dare to interrupt the happy group anyway? She did not fear being yelled at. People raise their voices mostly to relieve their own tensions. And since, according to Ferdinand the watchman, Madam's husband beat her, she took her revenge out on the servants. Why feel resentful? It was far better to just accept it philosophically. But to be taken to task in front of others, strangers, that was worse than being slapped. So Carmen preferred to wait.

Also, Madam had the annoying habit of speaking to her daughter as if she were an adult.

'Françoise, sweetheart, what did you have to eat?' And little Françoise, while reciting for her mother, would delight in explaining that she had not eaten any dessert because the mandarins Carmen wanted to give her were rotten. And Madam would admonish Carmen for not having told her about it. Especially since she had already explained that without dessert the child might not get a well-balanced meal, and so on and so forth. Carmen would usually listen to it all, seriously. In her village, and over in Makélékélé, what mattered was that a child had a full belly and did not go hungry. If, in addition, they had to worry about a balanced diet, there would never be an end to it. Besides, Carmen must not forget to ask her mistress . . .

There was only one solution. Do as her own mother had done to get her to eat. With one hand she opened the child's mouth and with the other shoved in the piece of fruit. As expected, Françoise howled. She cried and choked with rage. From the hallway came hammer-like sounds on the tile floor – the footsteps of Madam who came running. Carmen had won.

'What's going on in here?'

'She doesn't want to eat, Madam.'

'Oh don't force her, poor little thing. Get her some grapes from the refrigerator. She likes grapes.'

Madam took the little girl's head in her hands and kissed her several times. Carmen went to get the European-style dessert. As she was returning, she crossed Madam in the hall and almost broached the subject that was on her mind. But it did not seem like quite the right moment.

Françoise ate the grapes with relish. They must be good because instead of being her usual, talkative self, she remained calm and quiet as she ate the fruit. One day Carmen would have to swipe some of them and see what they tasted like.

While the little girl ate, Carmen wiped the tears from her cheeks. In her heart she cared a great deal for this child. Carmen had been with her since she was two months old and had practically brought her up. Françoise was as much her daughter as Madam's. Even if she quit her job, or Madam fired her, she would not be able to resist returning from time to time to see how Françoise had grown.

Then Carmen took the little girl to spend a penny, changed her, and put her to bed. By then it was 7.30. Night had fallen and she would still have an hour's walk to reach Makélékélé. But Françoise did not want her maid to leave. She clung to her annoying routine of wanting Carmen to sing her to sleep with a song.

> 'Nguè kélé mwana ya mboté,
> Sleep baby sleep,
> Sleep baby sleep.'

After that she had to sing another. Usually the child would fall asleep during the second song but that evening it took three. While Carmen sang, her thoughts were elsewhere. She thought about Françoise whom she loved as much as her son, a child of the same age yet so different. Françoise was the picture of health, while her son had come close to death several times already. Nothing intimidated Françoise, she was comfortable speaking with grown-ups, ordered about the servants and already showed a certain fussiness in her choice of clothes. Her Hector did not dare to speak. He was shy and withdrawn with strangers. His unhappiness already showed in his eyes. Yet both children were of the same generation. They spoke the same language but would they be able to understand each other? Carmen did not think this jealously. No, she would like Hector to be 'well brought up', but how could that possibly be? Society and human nature would have to change.

That morning she had been very tempted to stay home from work. All night long the poor little fellow had cried. He complained of a stomach ache. He had diarrhoea and vomited at least three times. The first time seemed to relieve him, but the last brought something greenish up from his little stomach. Then his stomach continued to contract spasmodically and nothing more came up. The child was clearly in pain. His breathing was laboured, his forehead covered with sweat. She was very frightened and thought of the two children she had already lost. She even panicked. She had almost awakened her mother, asleep in the same compound. But she restrained herself. Her mother would have taken him immediately to the fetishist. That was how it happened with the other two. And they died. Yet each time she paid the equivalent of her own earnings. And after their deaths it was worse. The fetishist concluded she kept losing her children because for five years she had been refusing to marry the man her parents had chosen for her. And, in addition to her grief, she was obliged to suffer the nonsense of a relentless succession of old hags who harped on the subject, and tried to pressure her into yielding and giving in to either the will of God, the ancestors, the spirits, or her poor children. She should marry Kitonga Flavien and then everything would be all right again. Wasn't he a good catch? Besides his job as a government chauffeur, he was his own boss after work. He owned four taxis, a shop and a bar in Ouenze-Indochina. Kitonga would support her, she wouldn't have to work any longer. Besides, he already had two wives. One at Bacongo and the other who ran the bar at Ouenze.

While she contemplated all this, her son called. He wanted to sleep on her mat. He was afraid to be alone. Would he last until morning? When some children are sick their parents can immediately pick up the phone, dial a number and go straight to the doctor who does whatever is needed, or reassures them. But not poor people! The closest dispensaries are closed at night. And at the hospital we are received by a nurse who is rude and makes a fuss because we dared to wake him. As for going to a doctor, well, folks who live in the better parts of town won't open their doors at night to just anyone. Besides, she is letting her imagination run wild. A visit to a private doctor costs money.

Finally, at dawn, the child fell asleep. As for Carmen, she had to get up and go to work. Everyday she must walk two hours from Makélékélé to Mipla. Since her mistress wants her to be there before 7.30, it's easy to calculate ...

Despite her exhaustion she did not want to stay in bed. But neither did she want to go to work that morning. She would have preferred to go to the hospital and find out exactly what was wrong with Hector. Whenever he was ill, Carmen did not like to leave him alone. Her heart was not at ease. Once she tried to take him along to work, but Madam had made it plain that she was not being paid to care for her own son but for Françoise. Carmen knew that her mother and the other female relatives would take him to see a doctor. The tribal family is large and a child, no matter what happens, is never alone. But nonetheless, she believed that a child is best off being brought up by its mother. And those we have brought into the world need us most of all when they are sick.

But if she had devoted the day to her son, she would have been fired and then how would they manage? She had already missed work twice that month. The first time she really had been sick and had spent two feverish days on her mat. The second time was for a funeral. Madam was very angry.

'Carmen, I have had just about enough! Each time I need you, you aren't here. It almost seems as if you do it on purpose. You choose to stay home the very days I've made plans. My dear woman, I'm warning you now. If you miss one more day this month, you'll have to look for work elsewhere.'

How could she explain? Carmen tried her best. But white people, they think that whenever we don't come to work, it's because we're lazy.

And today she came to work despite Hector being so ill. At noon her sister sent word that the doctor had prescribed some medicine. It was always the same old story. How would she pay for it? Yet Hector must be cured.

And that evening, there she was, singing for a little girl who had everything, and whose parents were playing cards with other ladies and gentlemen.

When Françoise had fallen asleep, Carmen went to wait in the kitchen until the guests had finished their game of bridge. She spent the time talking to Ferdinand, the old watchman. Those were moments she generally enjoyed. It lightened her spirits, eased her worry. They exchanged gossip on the shortcomings of their employers. Usually when Ferdinand described things he had seen, he would mimic them and Carmen would laugh. That evening, however, she remained serious and Ferdinand remarked on it.

Finally Madam came into the kitchen.

'Haven't you left yet Carmen?'

It was the most difficult moment. 'Madam, I need some money.'

'Again? But I paid you only ten days ago.'

'My son is sick. He needs medicine.'

'Listen to that, just listen to that! So I am now the public welfare fund. They have children without a husband and then they can't manage to take care of them!'

'Madam, white people say that ...'

'So your child is sick? Well, it's because you don't listen to me. I've told you again and again that you must feed him properly. Did you do it?'

'No, Madam.'

'No, of course not. It's easier to fill his stomach with your rotten old *manioc*.'

What could Carmen answer? That she had tried the diet Madam suggested but it was beyond her means. It seemed that Madam did not realise how in one week she spent three times Carmen's monthly salary just to feed her husband, her daughter, herself and their cat. If the maid had reminded her of that, she would have been fired for insolence.

'But anyway, I don't have any cash at home this evening. When will you natives understand that money doesn't grow on trees? When will you learn to put money aside and save?'

And Madam continued speaking like that for a long time. Carmen did not understand all she said. When people speak French too rapidly, she doesn't have time to translate it all in her mind, so she just tunes out and nods her head, as she did at that moment. Had that perhaps softened Madam? In any case, she gave her some aspirin and promised her 500 francs the following day.

So finally black Carmen left. She walked all the way

back to Makélékélé. It was far from Mipla to Makélékélé. As far as from her native village to where she was sent to school. It left plenty of time for thought.

Carmen wanted to run, she felt so strongly that Hector needed her. But after not having slept the whole night, and eating nothing but a slice of *manioc* for lunch, she could not run. Suddenly she felt that Hector was calling her.

Poor little thing. 'When he grows up, will he love me? To support us both I must leave him alone all day long. Maybe he'll resent it. I regret having left him without medical care so long. But I had faith in the white man's medicine and in his good will. If Mamma suggests I take him to the fetishist tonight, I won't be able to refuse any longer.'

And she thought about all Madam had said. They would never really understand each other. Carmen spent more time with her mistress than with her own son. Madam entrusted her daughter to Carmen in complete confidence. And yet Carmen could not understand Madam's reactions nor could Madam imagine what was going on in her maid's head, or the difficulties of her world. She considered Carmen an irresponsible and frivolous girl.

How does she expect me to save money on 5000 francs a month? Last month she only paid me 4000. For six months now she has been keeping back 500 francs a month to help repay the cost of the watch I bought. It was my only extravagance. Then I had to give 1000 francs to the *tontine*[1] of our community, 1000 francs to my mother, 1000 francs to pay for the trip home of my aunt and cousins who had moved in with us for a

---

[1] a community-based method of saving

month. I had only 1000 francs left. And what is 1000 francs? Madam spends that much on food every day.

Cars passed by in the poorly lit streets. Those that came towards Carmen blinded her with their headlights. Those that arrived from behind barely missed hitting her. And no one stopped to give her a lift. Yet she knew that at least half of the cars were driven by blacks like herself. In today's world, each to his own.

Oh, if only Madam would remember to give her money for the medicine tomorrow.

As she approached Biza Street, the cry of women's voices raised in the night reached her:

> '*Mwana mounou mê kouenda hé!*
> *Hector hé,*
> *Mwana mounou mê kouenda hé.*'

She understood that medicine or fetishist, it was too late.

> 'Oh my son has gone away!
> Oh my Hector,
> Oh my son has gone away.'

The Ultimate Safari

by Nadine Gordimer

'THE AFRICAN ADVENTURE LIVES ON ... YOU CAN DO IT!
THE ULTIMATE SAFARI OR EXPEDITION WITH LEADERS
WHO KNOW AFRICA.'

Travel advertisement, *Observer*, 27 November 1988

That night our mother went to the shop and she didn't
come back. Ever. What happened? I don't know. My
father also had gone away one day and never come
back; but he was fighting in the war. We were in the war,
too, but we were children, we were like our grandmother and grandfather, we didn't have guns. The
people my father was fighting – the bandits, they are
called by our government – ran all over the place and
we ran away from them like chickens chased by dogs.
We didn't know where to go. Our mother went to the
shop because someone said you could get some oil for
cooking. We were happy because we hadn't tasted oil
for a long time; perhaps she got the oil and someone
knocked her down in the dark and took that oil from
her. Perhaps she met the bandits. If you meet them,
they will kill you. Twice they came to our village and we
ran and hid in the bush and when they'd gone we came
back and found they had taken everything; but the
third time they came back there was nothing to take, no
oil, no food, so they burned the thatch and the roofs of
our houses fell in. My mother found some pieces of tin

and we put those up over part of the house. We were waiting there for her that night she never came back.

We were frightened to go out, even to do our business, because the bandits did come. Not into our house – without a roof it must have looked as if there was no one in it, everything gone – but all through the village. We heard people screaming and running. We were afraid even to run, without our mother to tell us where. I am the middle one, the girl, and my little brother clung against my stomach with his arms round my neck and his legs round my waist like a baby monkey to its mother. All night my first-born brother kept in his hand a broken piece of wood from one of our burnt house-poles. It was to save himself if the bandits found him.

We stayed there all day. Waiting for her. I don't know what day it was; there was no school, no church any more in our village, so you didn't know whether it was a Sunday or a Monday.

When the sun was going down, our grandmother and grandfather came. Someone from our village had told them we children were alone, our mother had not come back. I say 'grandmother' before 'grandfather' because it's like that: our grandmother is big and strong, not yet old, and our grandfather is small, you don't know where he is, in his loose trousers, he smiles but he hasn't heard what you're saying, and his hair looks as if he's left it full of soap suds. Our grandmother took us – me, the baby, my first-born brother, our grandfather – back to her house and we were all afraid (expect the baby, asleep on our grandmother's back) of meeting the bandits on the way. We waited a long time at our grandmother's place. Perhaps it was a month. We were hungry. Our mother never came. While we were waiting for her to fetch us, our grandmother had no food for us, no food for our grandfather and herself. A woman with milk in her breasts gave us some for my little brother, although at our house he used to eat porridge, same as we did. Our grandmother took us to look for wild spinach but everyone else in the village did the same and there wasn't a leaf left.

Our grandfather, walking a little behind some young men, went to look for our mother but didn't find her. Our grandmother cried with other women and I sang the hymns with them. They brought a little food – some beans – but after two days there was nothing again. Our grandfather used to have three sheep and a cow and a vegetable garden but the bandits had long ago taken the sheep and the cow, because they were hungry, too; and when planting time came our grandfather had no seed to plant.

So they decided – our grandmother did; our grandfather made little noises and rocked from side to side, but she took no notice – we would go away. We children were pleased. We wanted to go away from where our mother wasn't and where we were hungry. We wanted to go where there were no bandits and there was food. We were glad to think there must be such a place; away.

Our grandmother gave her church clothes to someone in exchange for some dried mealies[1] and she boiled them and tied them in a rag. We took them with us when we went and she thought we would get water from the rivers but we didn't come to any river and we got so thirsty we had to turn back. Not all the way to our grandparents' place but to a village where there was a pump. She opened the basket where she carried some clothes and the mealies and she sold her shoes to buy a

[1] corn-cob

big plastic container for water. I said, *Gogo*, how will you go to church now even without shoes, but she said we had a long journey and too much to carry. At that village we met other people who were also going away. We joined them because they seemed to know where that was better than we did.

To get there we had to go through the Kruger Park. We knew about the Kruger Park. A kind of whole country of animals – elephants, lions, jackals, hyenas, hippos, crocodiles, all kinds of animals. We had some of them in our own country, before the war (our grandfather remembers; we children weren't born yet) but the bandits kill the elephants and sell their tusks, and the bandits and our soldiers have eaten all the buck. There was a man in our village without legs – a crocodile took them off, in our river; but all the same our country is a country of people, not animals. We knew about the Kruger Park because some of our men used to leave home to work there in the places where white people came to stay and look at the animals.

So we started to go away again. There were women and other children like me who had to carry the small ones on their backs when the women got tired. A man led us into the Kruger Park: are we there yet, are we there yet, I kept asking our grandmother. Not yet, the man said, when she asked him for me. He told us we had to take a long way to get round the fence, which he explained would kill you, roast off your skin the moment you touched it, like the wires high up on poles that give electric light in our towns. I've seen that sign of a head without ears or skin or hair on an iron box at the mission hospital we used to have before it was blown up.

When I asked the next time, they said we'd been walking in the Kruger Park for an hour. But it looked just like the bush we'd been walking through all day, and we hadn't seen any animals except the monkeys and birds which live around us at home, and a tortoise that, of course, couldn't get away from us. My first-born brother and the other boys brought it to the man so it could be killed and we could cook and eat it. He let it go because he told us we could not make a fire; all the time we were in the Park we must not make a fire because the smoke would show we were there. Police, wardens, would come and send us back where we came from. He said we must move like animals among the animals, away from the roads, away from the white people's camps. And at that moment I heard – I'm sure I was the first to hear – cracking branches and the sound of something parting grasses and I almost squealed because I thought it was the police, wardens – the people he was telling us to look out for – who had found us already. And it was an elephant, and another elephant, and more elephants, big blots of dark moved wherever you looked between the trees. They were curling their trunks round the red leaves of the mopane trees and stuffing them into their mouths. The babies leaned against their mothers. The almost grown-up ones wrestled like my first-born brother with his friends – only they used trunks instead of arms. I was so interested I forgot to be afraid. The man said we should just stand still and be quiet while the elephants passed. They passed very slowly because elephants are too big to need to run from anyone.

The buck ran from us. They jumped so high they seemed to fly. The wart-hogs stopped dead, when they heard us, and swerved off the way a boy in our village used to zigzag on the bicycle his father had brought back from the mines. We followed the animals to where they drank. When they had gone, we went to their waterholes. We were never thirsty without finding water, but the animals ate, ate all the time. Whenever you saw them they were eating, grass, trees, roots. And there was nothing for us. The mealies were finished. The only food we could eat was what the baboons ate, dry little figs full of ants, that grow along the branches of the trees at the rivers. It was hard to be like the animals.

When it was very hot during the day we would find lions lying asleep. They were the colour of the grass and we didn't see them at first but the man did, and he led us back and a long way round where they slept. I wanted to lie down like the lions. My little brother was getting thin but he was very heavy. When our grandmother looked for me, to put him on my back, I tried not to see. My first-born brother stopped talking; and when we rested he had to be shaken to get up again, as if he was just like our grandfather, he couldn't hear. I saw flies crawling on our grandmother's face and she didn't brush them off; I was frightened. I picked up a palm leaf and chased them.

We walked at night as well as by day. We could see the fires where the white people were cooking in the camps and we could smell the smoke and the meat. We watched the hyenas with their backs that slope as if they're ashamed, slipping through the bush after the smell. If one turned its head, you saw it had big brown shining eyes like our own, when we looked at each other in the dark. The wind brought voices in our own language from the compounds where the people who work in the camps live. A woman among us wanted to go to them at night and ask them to help us. They can give us the food from the dustbins, she said, she started wailing and our grandmother had to grab her and put a hand over her mouth. The men who led us had told us that we must keep out of the way of our people who worked at the Kruger Park; if they helped us they would lose their work. If they saw us, all they could do was pretend we were not there; they had seen only animals.

Sometimes we stopped to sleep for a little while at night. We slept close together. I don't know which night it was – because we were walking, walking, any time, all the time – we heard the lions very near. Not groaning loudly the way they did far off. Panting, like we do when we run, but it's a different kind of panting: you can hear they're not running, they're waiting, somewhere near. We all rolled closer together, on top of each other, the ones on the edge fighting to get into the middle. I was squashed against a woman who smelled bad because she was afraid but I was glad to hold tight on to her. I prayed to God to make the lions take someone on the edge and go. I shut my eyes not to see the tree from which a lion might jump right into the middle of us, where I was. The man who led us jumped up instead, and beat on the tree with a dead branch. He had taught us never to make a sound but he shouted. He shouted at the lions like a drunk man shouting at nobody in our village. The lions went away. We heard them groaning, shouting back at him from far off.

We were tired, so tired. My first-born brother and the man had to lift our grandfather from stone to stone where we found places to cross the rivers. Our grand-mother is strong but her feet were bleeding. We could not carry the basket on our heads any longer, we couldn't carry anything except my little brother. We left our things under a bush. As long as our bodies get there, our grandmother said. Then we ate some wild fruit we didn't know from home and our stomachs ran. We were in the grass called elephant grass because it is nearly as tall as an elephant, that day we had those pains, and our grandfather couldn't just get down in front of people like my little brother, he went off into the grass to be on his own. We had to keep up, the man who led us always kept telling us, we must catch up, but we asked him to wait for our grandfather.

So everyone waited for our grandfather to catch up. But he didn't. It was the middle of the day; insects were singing in our ears and we couldn't hear him moving through the grass. We couldn't see him because the grass was so high and he was so small. But he must have been somewhere there inside his loose trousers and his shirt that was torn and our grandmother couldn't sew because she had no cotton. We knew he couldn't have gone far because he was weak and slow. We all went to look for him, but in groups, so we too wouldn't be hidden from each other in that grass. It got into our eyes and noses; we called him softly but the noise of the insects must have filled the little space left for hearing in his ears. We looked and looked but we couldn't find him. We stayed in that long grass all night. In my sleep I found him curled round in a place he had tramped down for himself, like the places we'd seen where the buck hide their babies.

When I woke up he still wasn't anywhere. So we looked again, and by now there were paths we'd made by going through the grass many times, it would be easy for him to find us if we couldn't find him. All that day we just sat and waited. Everything is very quiet when the sun is on your head, inside your head, even if you lie, like the animals, under the trees. I lay on my back and saw those ugly birds with hooked beaks and plucked necks flying round and round above us. We had passed them often where they were feeding on the bones of dead animals, nothing was ever left there for us to eat.

Round and round, high up and then lower down and then high again. I saw their necks poking to this side and that. Flying round and round. I saw our grandmother, who sat up all the time with my little brother on her lap, was seeing them, too.

In the afternoon the man who led us came to our grandmother and told her the other people must move on. He said, If their children don't eat soon they will die.

Our grandmother said nothing.

I'll bring you water before we go, he told her.

Our grandmother looked at us, me, my first-born brother, and my little brother on her lap. We watched the other people getting up to leave. I didn't believe the grass would be empty, all around us, where they had been. That we would be alone in this place, the Kruger Park, the police or the animals would find us. Tears came out of my eyes and nose on to my hands but our grandmother took no notice. She got up, with her feet apart the way she puts them when she is going to lift firewood, at home in our village, she swung my little brother on to her back, tied him in her cloth – the top of her dress was torn and her big breasts were showing but there was nothing in them for him. She said, Come.

So we left the place with the long grass. Left behind. We went with the others and the man who led us. We started to go away, again.

There's a very big tent, bigger than a church or a school, tied down to the ground. I didn't understand that was what it would be, when we got there, away. I saw a thing like that the time our mother took us to the town because she heard our soldiers were there and she wanted to ask them if they knew where our father was. In that tent, people were praying and singing. This one is blue and white like that one but it's not for praying and singing, we live in it with other people who've come from our country. Sister from the clinic says we're 200 without counting the babies, and we have new babies, some were born on the way through the Kruger Park.

Inside, even when the sun is bright it's dark and there's a kind of whole village in there. Instead of houses each family has a little place closed off with sacks or cardboard from boxes – whatever we can find – to show the other families it's yours and they shouldn't come in even though there's no door and no windows and no thatch, so that if you're standing up and you're not a small child you can see into everybody's house. Some people have even made paint from ground rocks and drawn designs on the sacks.

Of course, there really is a roof – the tent is the roof, far, high up. It's like a sky. It's like a mountain and we're inside it; through the cracks paths of dust lead down, so thick you think you could climb them. The tent keeps off the rain overhead but the water comes in at the sides and in the little streets between our places – you can only move along them one person at a time – the small kids like my little brother play in the mud. You have to step over them. My little brother doesn't play. Our grandmother takes him to the clinic when the doctor comes on Mondays. Sister says there's something wrong with his head, she thinks it's because we didn't have enough food at home. Because of the war. Because our father wasn't there. And then because he was so hungry in the Kruger Park. He likes just to lie about on our grandmother all day, on her lap or against her somewhere and he looks at us and looks at us. He wants to ask something but you can see he can't. If I tickle him he may just smile. The clinic gives us special powder to make into porridge for him and perhaps one day he'll be all right.

When we arrived we were like him – my first-born brother and I. I can hardly remember. The people who lived in the village near the tent took us to the clinic, it's where you have to sign that you've come – away, through the Kruger Park. We sat on the grass and everything was muddled. One Sister was pretty with her hair straightened and beautiful high-heeled shoes and she brought us the special powder. She said we must mix it with water and drink it slowly. We tore the packets open with our teeth and licked it all up, it stuck round my mouth and I sucked it from my lips and fingers. Some other children who had walked with us vomited. But I only felt everything in my belly moving, the stuff going down and around like a snake, and hiccups hurt me. Another Sister called us to stand in the line on the veranda of the clinic but we couldn't. We sat all over the place there, falling against each other: the Sisters helped each of us up by the arm and then stuck a needle in it. Other needles drew our blood into tiny bottles. This was against sickness, but I didn't understand, every time my eyes dropped closed I thought I was walking, the grass was long. I saw the elephants, I didn't know we were away.

But our grandmother was still strong, she could still stand up, she knows how to write and she signed for us. Our grandmother got us this place in the tent against one of the sides, it's the best kind of place there because although the rain comes in, we can lift the flap when the weather is good and then the sun shines on us, the smells in the tent go out. Our grandmother knows a woman here who showed her where there is good grass for sleeping mats, and our grandmother made some for us. Once every month the food truck comes to the clinic. Our grandmother takes along one of the cards she signed and when it has been punched we get a sack of mealie meal. There are wheelbarrows to take it back to the tent: my first-born brother does this for her and then he and the other boys have races, steering the empty wheelbarrows back to the clinic. Sometimes he's lucky and a man who's bought beer in the village gives him money to deliver it – though that's not allowed, you're supposed to take that wheelbarrow straight back to the Sisters. He buys a cold drink and shares it with me if I catch him. On another day, every month, the church leaves a pile of old clothes in the clinic yard. Our grandmother has another card to get punched, and then we can choose something: I have two dresses, two pants and a jersey, so I can go to school.

The people in the village have let us join their school. I was surprised to find they speak our language; our grandmother told me, That's why they allow us to stay on their land. Long ago, in the time of our fathers, there was no fence that kills you, there was no Kruger Park between them and us, we were the same people under our own king, right from our village we left to this place we've come to.

Now that we've been in the tent so long – I have turned eleven and my little brother is nearly three although he is so small, only his head is big, he's not come right in it yet – some people have dug up the bare ground around the tent and planted beans and mealies and cabbage. The old men weave branches to put up fences round their gardens. No one is allowed to look for work in the towns but some of the women have found work in the village and can buy things. Our grandmother, because she's still strong, finds work where people are building houses – in this village the people build nice houses with bricks and cement, not mud like we used to have at our home. Our grandmother carries bricks for these people and fetches baskets of stones on her head. And so she has money to buy sugar and tea and milk and soap. The store gave her a calender she has hung up on our flap of the tent. I am clever at school and she collected advertising paper people throw away outside the store and covered my school-books with it. She makes my first-born brother and me do our homework every afternoon before it gets dark because there is no room except to lie down, close together, just as we did in the Kruger Park, in our place in the tent, and candles are expensive. Our grandmother hasn't been able to buy herself a pair of shoes for church yet, but she has bought black school shoes and polish to clean them with for my first-born brother and me. Every morning, when people are getting up in the tent, the babies are crying, people are pushing each other at the taps outside and some children are already pulling the crusts of porridge off the pots we ate from last night, my first-born brother and I clean our shoes. Our grandmother makes us sit on our mats with our legs straight out so she can look carefully at our shoes to make sure we have done it properly. No other children in the tent have real school shoes. When we three look at them it's as if we are in a real house again, with no war, no away.

Some white people came to take photographs of our people living in the tent – they said they were making a film, I've never seen what that is though I know about it. A white woman squeezed into our space and asked our grandmother questions which were told to us in our language by someone who understands the white woman's.

'How long have you been living like this?'

'She means here?' Our grandmother said. 'In this tent, two years and one month.'

'And what do you hope for the future?'

'Nothing. I'm here.'

'But for your children?'

'I want them to learn so that they can get good jobs and money.'

'Do you hope to go back to your own country?'

'I will not go back.'

'But when the war is over – you won't be allowed to stay here? Don't you want to go home?'

I didn't think our grandmother wanted to speak again. I didn't think she was going to answer the white woman. The white woman put her head on one side and smiled at us.

Our grandmother looked away from her and spoke. 'There is nothing. No home.'

Why does our grandmother say that? Why? I'll go back. I'll go back through that Kruger Park. After the war, if there are no bandits any more, our mother may be waiting for us. And maybe when we left our grandfather, he was only left behind, he found his way somehow, slowly, through the Kruger Park, and he'll be there. They'll be home, and I'll remember them.

Kgotla

by Bessie Head

No day passed without its news, and in the early
morning the old men shuffled their way towards the
central kgotla[1] of the village, their walking-sticks lightly
tapping the ground. Two regular kgotla-goers, Kelapile
and Thatayarona, met each other just as they were
about to enter the wide, semicircular wooden enclosure
of the kgotla. They each clasped a low, wooden kgotla
stool in each left hand and were dressed in their heavy
greatcoats as there was a chill in the air. Kelapile was
already stooped with age and somewhat absent-minded.
Thatayarona was thin, upright, still with a spring in his
walk and a loud, authoritative voice that sounded like a
deep drum in his chest. They often dominated kgotla
affairs together: Kelapile, for his wily insight into
human nature; Thatayarona, because he liked to make
his voice heard. After they had greeted each other,
Kelapile asked:

'What could be the matter under discussion today,
Thatayarona? I did not attend afternoon kgotla
yesterday as I felt ill, so I do not know the proceedings
for today.'

'We heard there was going to be a government pronouncement about a new way of gathering tax,'
Thatayarona boomed. 'But I doubt it can be done today
because all the headmen have not yet been informed

[1] an assembly of village elders whose guidance is respected

101

that they should attend kgotla. This news suddenly arrived late in the afternoon, so the pronouncement may be given a day or two later ...'

They set their stools down near the wooden palings and for a time the two men sat, lost in their own thoughts. Things started leisurely at the kgotla because the chief in charge of it was now old and very ill and given to turning up on duty at any old time.

Behind the kgotla, an administrative block had been set up to modernise village life. It fussed about schools, boreholes, roads, development and progress; energetic young clerks dashed from one department to another, their hands filled with bureaucratic paperwork. They had no time to listen to the twitter of birds in the ancient shady trees that surrounded the kgotla, but the two worlds daily travelled side by side and the bureaucratic world was fast devouring up the activities of the ancient, rambling kgotla world. They had taken over, from the chief, the duty of land allocation, water rights and things like that, but they hadn't yet taken over people's affairs – the kgotla was still the people's place. It was the last stronghold where people could make their anguish and disputes heard, where nothing new could be said about human nature – it had all been said since time immemorial and it was all of the same pattern, repeating itself from generation unto generation. There, at the kgotla, it wasn't so important to resolve human problems as to discuss around them, to pontificate, to generalise, to display wit, wisdom, wealth of experience or depth of thought. All this made the kgotla world a holy world that moved at its own pace and time and two old men sat dreaming by themselves that early morning.

They stirred a little as a group of people slowly approached the kgotla. As they came near, the two old men noted that the slow movement of the group was due to the fact that they had a blind man in their midst. He was very tall and walked with his hands stiffly at his sides, independent of aid from his companions, but he walked awkwardly with loud, heavy-paced footsteps, lifting his feet too high off the ground each time. He stared ahead of him with wide-open, astonished brown eyes that saw nothing, and every now and then he broke into an angelic, white-toothed smile. The blind man's companions were all women and they sorted themselves out into various groups as they sat down on the ground. A young and good-looking woman, together with an old woman who had her head heavily bandaged, sat on the right side of the blind man; and a group of four women huddled together on his left side. The two old men looked at this strange gathering of people with interest and could make nothing of what their problem could be, but it looked like being an interesting day. Kelapile bent over and whispered to Thatayarona:

'Women are always poking at each other but I wonder who could have tried to kill the old mother?'

Thatayarona chuckled with delight. He already imagined his voice booming over the assembly with witty observations. Just then the old chief arrived in his van and made straight for the kgotla. A number of old men like Kelapile and Thatayarona, who acted as his assessors, also appeared and settled themselves on stools near him. The chief, who these days normally prepared himself to doze when proceedings bored him, also looked at the gathering with interest.

'I believe this case comes from Goo-ra-mere ward,' he began briskly. 'I have received a report about it from headman Serekete who says it has so many complications, he just does not know where to begin.' He paused and asked: 'Who is the owner of this case?'

'I am,' the good-looking young woman said quietly.

'Speak then, let us hear what you have to say.'

'It was four years ago that my husband here, Gobosamang, came to Bulawayo[2] to attend at the school for the blind. I was a helper at the school. I liked all his ways at that time, so when he proposed marriage to me, I accepted him. During the year we lived together in my country we were happy and the marriage prospered. It was my husband's idea that we return to his country, but since then nothing has gone right with the marriage. It's the first time I have seen jealousy and spite such as exists in this village and people here have no love or respect for a foreign person. My name is Rose but I hear myself referred to as "that Sindebele woman". It was not long after we arrived that I began to see that people had poisoned my husband against me. Their words to him were that I was taking lovers behind his back and not a day passed when he was not quarrelling with me about this matter. What does it help to say: "The words of those people are not the truth." He cannot see and is dependent on all the poison which is poured into his ears by others. For three years I have lived in misery and the day came when I could stand this strife no more. I thought: "People's jealousy for me is burning my back like a live coal resting there. I shall go back to my own people." I returned to my people but this did not please them because when we married, as is our custom, Gobosamang had offered my people cattle. They feared they would have to return the gifts so they were not pleased by my reappearance. "Oh no," they said, "return to the husband. Jealousy like that is a natural thing. After all, you are a beautiful woman." But I rested

[2] a city in Zimbabwe

there for three months to settle my mind. On my return I found that another woman now occupied my yard and my husband. She had been recently bereaved of her own husband and had made haste to take another. She claims that she offered Gobosamang all her money and worldly goods, which he has already eaten, and she demands that the money and goods be returned. For some days she would not remove herself from the yard and it was only when she had assaulted Gobosamang's mother that he removed her by force.'

Appreciative nods from the chief and his assessors greeted this simple and straightforward statement from the woman Rose, but it was essential to bring out all the points of the case before any comment could be made.

'We have heard you, Rose,' the chief said, already deeply involved in the affair. He shifted his attention to the old woman with the heavily bandaged head: 'Now tell us mother what you have to say.'

'I am Galeboe Lentswe, the mother of Gobosamang here,' she began. 'My son has brought all this trouble on himself, with full awareness, so I have little sympathy for him. He left home for some time and returned with a good and beautiful wife, which was something people did not expect, as he is blind. The marriage filled everyone with wonder and people ever commented that Gobosamang was a lucky man indeed. Then I noticed that this very good luck had created a madness in my son's mind. He could not rest if the wife was not nearby: "Mother, is it not true that my wife has fallen in love with another man? That is what people tell me." He was very nervous about it and I used to pacify him: "No Gobosamang, she has just gone to draw water like any other wife. Besides no one is the owner of any other person, so you should not expect the wife to be tied to you, day and night." But nothing I could say would remove this madness from his head. By the time the wife ran away, I was exhausted. Gobosamang became very ill for a few days. The day I informed him that the wife had run away, he dropped to the ground in a dead faint. I thought he was finished and done for, but no, he stood up after two days and without one word to me, he walked out of the yard and returned a day later with that moswagadi[3] woman here, Tsietso. I was very shocked and afraid. I approached my son secretly and said: "Gobosamang, you cannot bring a moswagadi into the yard. You know that it is barely three months since her husband passed away and by custom you should not be having relations with a woman like that. You can die." It was as if my son were mad. He would not hear anything I had to say, so I kept quiet and left this unhealthy matter to pursue its course. After three months the wife returned. She said she had been forced by her people to return to her lawful husband and indeed she had her rightful place there as Gobosamang's wife. But do you think we could persuade that moswagadi to leave? She was put up to her rudeness by my son who chose to deliberately ignore his wife. Gobosamang's rightful wife and I were forced to share a hut while he continued to live with the moswagadi. Then, the other day, Gobosamang's wife wanted to make some fat cakes for the evening meal. She prepared the flour and everything, then noticed that there was no cooking fat in the house, so she went to the shop to buy some. On her return she found that the basin of flour had been thrown into a bucket of water: "Who has done this?" she asked. The moswagadi was there, looking at her like a snake. She laughed and said: "I'm sure I don't know." But I had seen it all, so I

[3] a woman recently bereaved of her husband

said: "Tsietso, you might have thought I was dozing here but I saw you throw the flour into the water-bucket. And I would advise you to watch your manners and not have too much to say for yourself in our yard. You are the person who is in trouble, not Rose." These were peaceful words, but to my surprise, Tsietso picked up a big stone and threw it at my head. It just missed. Not satisfied with that, she then grabbed me by the ears and pulled them hard. I have a pain in my head to this day. That was when Gobosamang agreed to remove that moswagadi from the yard.'

Trouble and damnation were piling up on the head of the blind man, Gobosamang, so attention next shifted to him.

'Gobosamang,' the chief said, with a surprised expression. 'Tell us if all these things that have so far been said about you are the truth.'

The blind man seemed to be thoroughly enjoying his predicament. That angelic white-toothed smile lit up his face.

'I have nothing to say for myself,' he said. 'I can see that I am in big trouble. But the truth has been spoken so far.'

The chief shook his head slowly expressing his amazement that a blind and handicapped man like Gobosamang could make such an impossible muddle of life. He next turned his attention to the group of four women huddled together.

'I suppose you are the people of Morule ward from which Tsietso comes,' he said. 'Headman Serekete told me that is the ward of Tsietso.'

'Yes, we are the people of Morule ward,' one of the women spoke up. 'And we have accompanied our child Tsietso here to see that justice is done by her at this court. She has given Gobosamang all her money and worldly goods under the false impression that they would start life together. We were surprised to find her cast back into her own yard penniless, and we want all the things she gave to Gobosamang returned.'

'I hear, people of Morule ward,' the chief said. 'Tsietso, tell us your side of the story.'

Tsietso, a tall, thin woman with a loud and vigorous voice looked at the ground with an offended air as she began to speak:

'I was minding my own business, mind you, when Gobosamang came weeping into my yard. "Tsietso," he said. "You are the only one who can understand my pain as you have only recently lost someone you love. My wife is gone and dead by now. I shall never see her again. Let us join our lives together and comfort each other." So I said: "Gobosamang, you know a year of mourning must pass before I can be cleansed and take another man. I am not available." And he said: "Oh, many people have broken custom and no harm has come to them. We don't believe such things any more." I know that as a fact too, that people have broken the custom of observing moswagadi and lived. The trouble with Gobosamang is that he appeals to the heart. He is like a small child who must be cared for and when I saw him weeping like that, my heart was filled with pity and I agreed to his proposal and went to live with him.'

'What are these goods you have given to Gobosamang?' the chief asked.

'I had R300.00[4] which I gave to Gobosamang,' she said. 'We were to use it for our life together. I gave Gobosamang the money on the understanding that his wife had departed for ever. He said we should buy cattle

---

[4] 300 Rands (South African money)

and improve the yard. We were planning all these things together when the wife returned.'

'Gobosamang,' the chief asked. 'Do you still have this R300.00?'

The terrible blind man still smiled: 'We have eaten all of it,' he said. 'Tsietso forgets that she has four children and how were we to feed them every day? I have no employment.'

The essentials of the case having been heard, the court relaxed from its position of attentive listening. It was now time for the assessors and the chief to make known their views on the case. Almost immediately Thatayarona's drum-like voice rolled over the assembly.

'This case has many profound points,' he said, importantly. 'Let us get back to the point made by Gobosamang's wife, Rose, about jealousy. It would appear as if the good lady has misunderstood our customs. There is no hatred for foreigners. Indeed, the contrary. It is well known from times past that a woman from a far-off place has more attraction than the woman who is known and at hand every day. We can see the course of events here. The men found virtue in the foreigner and they were ever commenting about it. This drove the women wild. They said: "Well now, what has Gobosamang's wife got that we haven't got?" So they decided to poison this happy marriage because they were wild with jealousy. It was wrong of Gobosamang to listen to this poison but then he appears a senseless man. That is my point.'

Not to be outdone in making good points, Kelapile followed fast on the heels of his friend with his own observations:

'We see another side of the old story today,' he said, with his profound air of wisdom. 'The forefathers said: "Jealousy starts from the eye." Today we have seen that it is equally troublesome to have no eyes with which to see. Gobosamang cannot see all the lovers his wife is said to possess and yet he is maddened by jealousy of them. A man with sense would merely observe on being told all these stories: "Well, I am blind. I don't see my wife's lovers, so why should they bother me?" But he is bothered. There is no peace anywhere, either for those who have eyes and for those who have not.'

After this profound statement on life itself, one of the more self-effacing of the assessors said meekly: 'We should not forget that an assault was made on the old mother here and Tsietso ought to explain herself as this is a serious offence.'

At this Tsietso burst into tears briefly.

'Gobosamang's mother would like herself to be known as a saint,' she said. 'But she has a venomous tongue. There was only misery there all the time I lived with Gobosamang. She treated me with scorn. I could not touch any of the household things and had to bring all my own utensils into the yard. A person who is hated is insulted every day, and so a fire built up in my heart against her. By the time I grabbed her by the ears, I no longer knew what I was doing as there was only hatred between us ...'

It was now time for the chief to pass judgement on the case. He bent his head and spoke as though he had considered all aspects of the matter at hand very carefully.

'Tsietso,' he said. 'The court well understands the complications of this case, but you have caused the old mother pain. She has felt a pain from your assault on her life and for that I fine you R20.00. Now you, Gobosamang, I order you to return the R300.00 you have taken from Tsietso. Also, from now on you are to live in peace with your own true wife. The grievances have been aired and understood, so we consider the matter settled now.'

The crazy blind man looked a little troubled at last.

'I have no way in which I can repay Tsietso the money I am ordered to pay,' he said earnestly. 'I have nothing.'

There was a brief silence. Everyone knew that that was ultimately the crux of the case and it might never be resolved. Then, in the silence, Rose, the wife of Gobosamang spoke very quietly:

'I can get a job in an office somewhere because I know how to do book-keeping. If Tsietso does not mind, we can then pay back the money owing to her, bit by bit.'

The whole assembly murmured its approval of this noble gesture and the court began to disperse as it was already near the lunch-hour. Thatayarona and Kelapile shuffled away together. As they walked along Kelapile nodded his head profoundly several times.

'I have seen a wonder today, Thatayarona,' he observed at last. 'The Sindebele woman fills me with wonder. You know very well that we can never settle cases at kgotla and this case looked impossible from the start. The forefathers were right when they said that the finest things often come from far-off places . . .'

The Return

by Ngugi Wa Thiong'o

The road was long. Whenever he took a step forward, little clouds of dust rose, whirled angrily behind him, and then slowly settled again. But a thin train of dust was left in the air, moving like smoke. He walked on, however, unmindful of the dust and ground under his feet. Yet with every step he seemed more and more conscious of the hardness and apparent animosity of the road. Not that he looked down; on the contrary, he looked straight ahead as if he would, any time now, see a familiar object that would hail him as a friend and tell him that he was near home. But the road stretched on.

He made quick, springing steps, his left hand dangling freely by the side of his once white coat, now torn and worn out. His right hand, bent at the elbow, held on to a string tied to a small bundle on his slightly drooping back. The bundle, well wrapped with a cotton cloth that had once been printed with red flowers now faded out, swung from side to side in harmony with the rhythm of his steps. The bundle held the bitterness and hardships of the years spent in detention camps. Now and then he looked at the sun on its homeward journey. Sometimes he darted quick side-glances at the small hedged strips of land which, with their sickly looking crops, maize, beans, and peas, appeared much as everything else did – unfriendly. The whole country was dull and seemed weary. To Kamau, this was nothing new. He remembered that, even before the Mau Mau emergency, the over-tilled Gikuyu holdings wore haggard looks in contrast to the sprawling green fields in the settled area.

A path branched to the left. He hesitated for a moment and then made up his mind. For the first time, his eyes brightened a little as he went along the path that would take him down the valley and then to the village. At last home was near and, with that realisation, the faraway look of a weary traveller seemed to desert him for a while. The valley and the vegetation along it were in deep contrast to the surrounding country. For here green bush and trees thrived. This could only mean one thing: Honia river still flowed. He quickened his steps as if he could scarcely believe this to be true till he had actually set his eyes on the river. It was there; it still flowed. Honia, where so often he had taken a bathe, plunging stark naked into its cool living water, warmed his heart as he watched its serpentine movement round the rocks and heard its slight murmurs. A painful exhilaration passed all over him, and for a moment he longed for those days. He sighed. Perhaps the river would not recognise in his hardened features that same boy to whom the riverside world had meant everything. Yet as he approached Honia, he felt more akin to it than he had felt to anything else since his release.

A group of women were drawing water. He was excited, for he could recognise one or two from his ridge. There was the middle-aged Wanjiku, whose deaf son had been killed by the Security Forces just before he himself was arrested. She had always been a darling of the village, having a smile for everyone and food for all. Would they receive him? Would they give him a 'hero's welcome'? He thought so. Had he not always been a favourite all along the Ridge? And had he not fought for the land? He wanted to run and shout: 'Here I am. I have come back to you.' But he desisted. He was a man.

'Is it well with you?' A few voices responded. The other women, with tired and worn features, looked at him mutely as if his greeting was of no consequence. Why! Had he been so long in the camp? His spirits were damped as he feebly asked: 'Do you not remember me?' Again they looked at him. They stared at him with cold, hard looks; like everything else, they seemed to be deliberately refusing to know or own him. It was Wanjiku who at last recognised him. But there was neither warmth nor enthusiasm in her voice as she said, 'Oh, is it you, Kamau? We thought you –' She did not continue. Only now he noticed something else – surprise? fear? He could not tell. He saw their quick glances dart at him and he knew for certain that a secret from which he was excluded bound them together.

'Perhaps I am no longer one of them!' he bitterly reflected. But they told him of the new village. The old village of scattered huts spread thinly over the Ridge was no more.

He left them, feeling embittered and cheated. The old village had not even waited for him. And suddenly he felt a strong nostalgia for his old home, friends and surroundings. He thought of his father, mother and – and – he dared not think about her. But for all that, Muthoni, just as she had been in the old days, came back to his mind. His heart beat faster. He felt desire and a warmth thrilled through him. He quickened his step. He forgot the village women as he remembered his wife. He had stayed with her for a mere two weeks; then he had been swept away by the Colonial Forces. Like many others, he had been hurriedly screened and then taken to detention without trial. And all that time he had thought of nothing but the village and his beautiful woman.

The others had been like him. They had talked of nothing but their homes. One day he was working next to another detainee from Muranga. Suddenly the detainee, Njoroge, stopped breaking stones. He sighed heavily. His worn-out eyes had a faraway look.

'What's wrong, man? What's the matter with you?' Kamau asked.

'It is my wife. I left her expecting a baby. I have no idea what has happened to her.'

Another detainee put in: 'For me, I left my woman with a baby. She had just been delivered. We were all happy. But on the same day, I was arrested ...'

And so they went on. All of them longed for one day – the day of their return home. Then life would begin anew.

Kamau himself had left his wife without a child. He had not even finished paying the bride-price. But now he would go, seek work in Nairobi, and pay off the remainder to Muthoni's parents. Life would indeed begin anew. They would have a son and bring him up in their own home. With these prospects before his eyes, he quickened his steps. He wanted to run – no, fly to hasten his return. He was now nearing the top of the hill. He wished he could suddenly meet his brothers and sisters. Would they ask him questions? He would, at any rate, not tell them all: the beating, the screening and the work on roads and in quarries with an askari[1] always nearby ready to kick him if he relaxed. Yes. He had suffered many humiliations, and he had not resisted. Was there any need? But his soul and all the

[1] African policeman

115

vigour of his manhood had rebelled and bled with rage and bitterness.

One day these wazungu[2] would go!

One day his people would be free! Then, then – he did not know what he would do. However, he bitterly assured himself no one would ever flout his manhood again.

He mounted the hill and then stopped. The whole plain lay below. The new village was before him – rows and rows of compact mud huts, crouching on the plain under the fast-vanishing sun. Dark blue smoke curled upwards from various huts, to form a dark mist that hovered over the village. Beyond, the deep, blood-red sinking sun sent out finger-like streaks of light that thinned outwards and mingled with the grey mist shrouding the distant hills.

In the village, he moved from street to street, meeting new faces. He enquired. He found his home. He stopped at the entrance to the yard and breathed hard and full. This was the moment of his return home. His father sat huddled up on a three-legged stool. He was now very aged and Kamau pitied the old man. But he had been spared – yes, spared to see his son's return –

'Father!'

The old man did not answer. He just looked at Kamau with strange vacant eyes. Kamau was impatient. He felt annoyed and irritated. Did he not see him? Would he behave like the women Kamau had met at the river?

In the street, naked and half-naked children were playing, throwing dust at one another. The sun had already set and it looked as if there would be moonlight.

[2] European people (in this context, the colonial British)

'Father, don't you remember me?' Hope was sinking in him. He felt tired. Then he saw his father suddenly start and tremble like a leaf. He saw him stare with unbelieving eyes. Fear was discernible in those eyes. His mother came, and his brothers too. They crowded around him. His aged mother clung to him and sobbed hard.

'I knew my son would come. I knew he was not dead.'

'Why, who told you I was dead?'

'That Karanja, son of Njogu.'

And then Kamau understood. He understood his trembling father. He understood the women at the river. But one thing puzzled him: he had never been in the same detention camp with Karanja. Anyway he had come back. He wanted now to see Muthoni. Why had she not come out? He wanted to shout, 'I have come, Muthoni; I am here.' He looked around. His mother understood him. She quickly darted a glance at her man and then simply said:

'Muthoni went away.'

Kamau felt something cold settle in his stomach. He looked at the village huts and the dullness of the land. He wanted to ask many questions but he dared not. He could not yet believe that Muthoni had gone. But he knew by the look of the women at the river, by the look of his parents, that she was gone.

'She was a good daughter to us,' his mother was explaining. 'She waited for you and patiently bore all the ills of the land. Then Karanja came and said that you were dead. Your father believed him. She believed him too and keened for a month. Karanja constantly paid us visits. He was of your Rika, you know. Then she got a child. We could have kept her. But where is the land? Where is the food? Ever since land consolidation, our last security was taken away. We let Karanja go with

117

her. Other women have done worse – gone to town. Only the infirm and the old have been left here.'

He was not listening; the coldness in his stomach slowly changed to bitterness. He felt bitter against all, all the people including his father and mother. They had betrayed him. They had leagued against him, and Karanja had always been his rival. Five years was admittedly not a short time. But why did she go? Why did they allow her to go? He wanted to speak. Yes, speak and denounce everything – the women at the river, the village and the people who dwelt there. But he could not. This bitter thing was choking him.

'You – you gave my own away?' he whispered.

'Listen, child, child –'

The big yellow moon dominated the horizon. He hurried away bitter and blind, and only stopped when he came to the Honia river.

And standing at the bank, he saw not the river, but his hopes dashed on the ground instead. The river moved swiftly, making ceaseless monotonous murmurs. In the forest the crickets and other insects kept up an incessant buzz. And above, the moon shone bright. He tried to remove his coat, and the small bundle he had held on to so firmly fell. It rolled down the bank and before Kamau knew what was happening, it was floating swiftly down the river. For a time he was shocked and wanted to retrieve it. What would he show his – Oh, had he forgotten so soon? His wife had gone. And the little things that had so strangely reminded him of her and that he had guarded all those years, had gone! He did not know why, but somehow he felt relieved. Thoughts of drowning himself dispersed. He began to put on his coat, murmuring to himself, 'Why should she have waited for me? Why should all the changes have waited for my return?'

The Rain Came

by Grace Ogot

The chief was still far from the gate when his daughter Oganda saw him. She ran to meet him. Breathlessly she asked her father, 'What is the news, great Chief? Everyone in the village is anxiously waiting to hear when it will rain.' Labong'o held out his hands for his daughter but he did not say a word. Puzzled by her father's cold attitude Oganda ran back to the village to warn the others that the chief was back.

The atmosphere in the village was tense and confused. Everyone moved aimlessly and fussed in the yard without actually doing any work. A young woman whispered to her co-wife, 'If they have not solved this rain business today, the chief will crack.' They had watched him getting thinner and thinner as the people kept on pestering him. 'Our cattle lie dying in the fields,' they reported. 'Soon it will be our children and then ourselves. Tell us what to do to save our lives, oh great Chief.' So the chief had daily prayed with the Almighty through the ancestors to deliver them from their distress.

Instead of calling the family together and giving them the news immediately, Labong'o went to his own hut, a sign that he was not to be disturbed. Having replaced the shutter, he sat in the dimly lit hut to contemplate.

It was no longer a question of being the chief of hunger-stricken people that weighed Labong'o's heart.

It was the life of his only daughter that was at stake. At the time when Oganda came to meet him, he saw the glittering chain shining around her waist. The prophecy was complete. 'It is Oganda, Oganda, my only daughter, who must die so young.' Labong'o burst into tears before finishing the sentence. The chief must not weep. Society had declared him the bravest of men. But Labong'o did not care any more. He assumed the position of a simple father and wept bitterly. He loved his people, the Luo, but what were the Luo for him without Oganda? Her life had brought a new life in Labong'o's world and he ruled better than he could remember. How would the spirit of the village survive his beautiful daughter? 'There are so many homes and so many parents who have daughters. Why choose this one? She is all I have.' Labong'o spoke as if the ancestors were there in the hut and he could see them face to face. Perhaps they were there, warning him to remember his promise on the day he was enthroned when he said aloud, before the elders, 'I will lay down life, if necessary, and the life of my household, to save this tribe from the hands of the enemy.' 'Deny! Deny!' he could hear the voice of his forefathers mocking him.

When Labong'o was consecrated chief he was only a young man. Unlike his father, he ruled for many years with only one wife. But people rebuked him because his only wife did not bear him a daughter. He married a second, a third, and a fourth wife. But they all gave birth to male children. When Labong'o married a fifth wife she bore him a daughter. They called her Oganda, meaning 'beans', because her skin was very fair. Out of Labong'o's twenty children, Oganda was the only girl. Though she was the chief's favourite, her mother's co-wives swallowed their jealous feelings and showered her with love. After all, they said, Oganda was a female child whose days in the royal family were numbered. She would soon marry at a tender age and leave the enviable position to someone else.

Never in his life had he been faced with such an impossible decision. Refusing to yield to the rain-maker's request would mean sacrificing the whole tribe, putting the interests of the individual above those of the society. More than that. It would mean disobeying the ancestors, and most probably wiping the Luo people from the surface of the earth. On the other hand, to let Oganda die as a ransom for the people would permanently cripple Labong'o spiritually. He knew he would never be the same chief again.

The words of Ndithi, the medicine man, still echoed in his ears. 'Podho, the ancestor of the Luo, appeared to me in a dream last night, and he asked me to speak to the chief and the people,' Ndithi had said to the gathering of tribesmen. 'A young woman who has not known a man must die so that the country may have rain. While Podho was still talking to me, I saw a young woman standing at the lakeside, her hands raised, above her head. Her skin was as fair as the skin of young deer in the wilderness. Her tall slender figure stood like a lonely reed at the river bank. Her sleepy eyes wore a sad look like that of a bereaved mother. She wore a gold ring on her left ear, and a glittering brass chain around her waist. As I still marvelled at the beauty of this young woman, Podho told me, "Out of all the women in this land, we have chosen this one. Let her offer herself a sacrifice to the lake monster! And on that day, the rain will come down in torrents. Let everyone stay at home on that day, lest he be carried away by the floods."'

Outside there was a strange stillness, except for the thirsty birds that sang lazily on the dying trees. The blinding midday heat had forced the people to retire to their huts. Not far away from the chief's hut, two guards were snoring away quietly. Labong'o removed his crown and the large eagle-head that hung loosely on his shoulders. He left the hut, and instead of asking Nyabog'o the messenger to beat the drum, he went straight and beat it himself. In no time the whole household had assembled under the siala tree where he usually addressed them. He told Oganda to wait a while in her grandmother's hut.

When Labong'o stood to address his household, his voice was hoarse and the tears choked him. He started to speak, but words refused to leave his lips. His wives and sons knew there was great danger. Perhaps their enemies had declared war on them. Labong'o's eyes were red, and they could see he had been weeping. At last he told them. 'One whom we love and treasure must be taken away from us. Oganda is to die.' Labong'o's voice was so faint, that he could not hear it himself. But he continued, 'The ancestors have chosen her to be offered as a sacrifice to the lake monster in order that we may have rain.'

They were completely stunned. As a confused murmur broke out, Oganda's mother fainted and was carried off to her own hut. But the other people rejoiced. They danced around singing and chanting, 'Oganda is the lucky one to die for the people. If it is to save the people, let Oganda go.'

In her grandmother's hut Oganda wondered what the whole family were discussing about her that she could not hear. Her grandmother's hut was well away from the chief's court and, much as she strained her ears, she could not hear what was said. 'It must be marriage,' she concluded. It was an accepted custom for the family to discuss their daughter's future marriage behind her back. A faint smile played on

Oganda's lips as she thought of the several young men who swallowed saliva at the mere mention of her name.

There was Kech, the son of a neighbouring clan elder. Kech was very handsome. He had sweet, meek eyes and a roaring laughter. He would make a wonderful father, Oganda thought. But they would not be a good match. Kech was a bit too short to be her husband. It would humiliate her to have to look down at Kech each time she spoke to him. Then she thought of Dimo, the tall young man who had already distinguished himself as a brave warrior and an outstanding wrestler. Dimo adored Oganda, but Oganda thought he would make a cruel husband, always quarrelling and ready to fight. No, she did not like him. Oganda fingered the glittering chain on her waist as she thought of Osinda. A long time ago when she was quite young Osinda had given her that chain, and instead of wearing it around her neck several times, she wore it round her waist where it could stay permanently. She heard her heart pounding so loudly as she thought of him. She whispered, 'Let it be you they are discussing, Osinda, the lovely one. Come now and take me away ...'

The lean figure in the doorway startled Oganda who was rapt in thought about the man she loved. 'You have frightened me, Grandma,' said Oganda laughing. 'Tell me, is it my marriage you were discussing? You can take it from me that I won't marry any of them.' A smile played on her lips again. She was coaxing the old lady to tell her quickly, to tell her they were pleased with Osinda.

In the open space outside the excited relatives were dancing and singing. They were coming to the hut now, each carrying a gift to put at Oganda's feet. As their singing got nearer Oganda was able to hear what they were saying: 'If it is to save the people, if it is to give us rain, let Oganda go. Let Oganda die for her people, and for her ancestors.' Was she mad to think that they were singing about her? How could she die? She found the lean figure of her grandmother barring the door. She could not get out. The look on her grandmother's face warned her that there was danger around the corner. 'Mother, it is not marriage then?' Oganda asked urgently. She suddenly felt panicky like a mouse cornered by a hungry cat. Forgetting that there was only one door in the hut Oganda fought desperately to find another exit. She must fight for her life. But there was none.

She closed her eyes, leapt like a wild tiger through the door, knocking her grandmother flat to the ground. There outside in mourning garments Labong'o stood motionless, his hands folded at the back. He held his daughter's hand and led her away from the excited crowd to the little red-painted hut where her mother was resting. Here he broke the news officially to his daughter.

For a long time the three souls who loved one another dearly sat in darkness. It was no good speaking. And even if they tried, the words could not have come out. In the past they had been like three cooking stones, sharing their burdens. Taking Oganda away from them would leave two useless stones which would not hold a cooking-pot.

News that the beautiful daughter of the chief was to be sacrificed to give the people rain spread across the country like wind. At sunset the chief's village was full of relatives and friends who had come to congratulate Oganda. Many more were on their way coming, carrying their gifts. They would dance till morning to keep her company. And in the morning they would prepare her a big farewell feast. All these relatives thought it a great honour to be selected by the spirits to die, in order that the society may live. 'Oganda's name will always remain a living name among us,' they boasted.

But was it maternal love that prevented Minya from rejoicing with the other women? Was it the memory of the agony and pain of child-birth that made her feel so sorrowful? Or was it the deep warmth and under-standing that passes between a suckling babe and her mother that made Oganda part of her life, her flesh? Of course it was an honour, a great honour, for her daughter to be chosen to die for the country. But what could she gain once her only daughter was blown away by the wind? There were so many other women in the land, why choose her daughter, her only child! Had human life any meaning at all – other women had houses full of children while she, Minya, had to lose her only child!

In the cloudless sky the moon shone brightly, and the numerous stars glittered with a bewitching beauty. The dancers of all age-groups assembled to dance before Oganda, who sat close to her mother, sobbing quietly. All these years she had been with her people she thought she understood them. But now she discovered that she was a stranger among them. If they loved her as they had always professed why were they not making any attempt to save her? Did her people really under-stand what it felt like to die young? Unable to restrain her emotions any longer, she sobbed loudly as her age-group got up to dance. They were young and beautiful and very soon they would marry and have their own children. They would have husbands to love and little huts for themselves. They would have reached maturity. Oganda touched the chain around her waist as she thought of Osinda. She wished Osinda was there too, among her friends. 'Perhaps he is ill,' she thought gravely. The chain comforted Oganda – she would die with it around her waist and wear it in the underground world.

In the morning a big feast was prepared for Oganda. The women prepared many different tasty dishes so that she could pick and choose. 'People don't eat after death,' they said. Delicious though the food looked, Oganda touched none of it. Let the happy people eat. She contented herself with sips of water from a little calabash.

The time for her departure was drawing near, and each minute was precious. It was a day's journey to the lake. She was to walk all night, passing through the great forest. But nothing could touch her, not even the denizens of the forest. She was already anointed with sacred oil. From the time Oganda received the sad news she had expected Osinda to appear any moment. But he was not there. A relative told her that Osinda was away on a private visit. Oganda realised that she would never see her beloved again.

In the afternoon the whole village stood at the gate to say good-bye and to see her for the last time. Her mother wept on her neck for a long time. The great chief in a mourning skin came to the gate bare-footed, and mingled with the people – a simple father in grief. He took off his wrist bracelet and put it on his daughter's wrist saying, 'You will always live among us. The spirit of our forefathers is with you.'

Tongue-tied and unbelieving Oganda stood there before the people. She had nothing to say. She looked at her home once more. She could hear her heart beating so painfully within her. All her childhood plans were coming to an end. She felt like a flower nipped in the bud never to enjoy the morning dew again. She looked at her weeping mother, and whispered, 'Whenever you want to see me, always look at the sunset. I will be there.'

Oganda turned southwards to start her trek to the lake. Her parents, relatives, friends and admirers stood at the gate and watched her go.

Her beautiful slender figure grew smaller and smaller till she mingled with the thin dry trees in the forest. As Oganda walked the lonely path that wound its way in the wilderness, she sang a song, and her own voice kept her company.

The ancestors have said Oganda must die
The daughter of the chief must be sacrificed,
When the lake monster feeds on my flesh.
The people will have rain.
Yes, the rain will come down in torrents.
And the floods will wash away the sandy beaches
When the daughter of the chief dies in the lake.
My age-group has consented
My parents have consented
So have my friends and relatives.
Let Oganda die to give us rain.
My age-group are young and ripe,
Ripe for womanhood and motherhood
But Oganda must die young,
Oganda must sleep with the ancestors.
Yes, rain will come down in torrents.

The red rays of the setting sun embraced Oganda, and she looked like a burning candle in the wilderness.

The people who came to hear her sad song were touched by her beauty. But they all said the same thing: 'If it is to save the people, if it is to give us rain, then be not afraid. Your name will forever live among us.'

At midnight Oganda was tired and weary. She could walk no more. She sat under a big tree, and having sipped water from her calabash, she rested her head on the tree trunk and slept.

When Oganda woke up in the morning the sun was high in the sky. After walking for many hours, she reached the *tong'*, a strip of land that separated the inhabited part of the country from the sacred place (*kar lamo*). No layman could enter this place and come out alive – only those who had direct contact with the spirits and the Almighty were allowed to enter this holy of holies. But Oganda had to pass through this sacred land on her way to the lake, which she had to reach at sunset.

A large crowd gathered to see her for the last time. Her voice was now hoarse and painful, but there was no need to worry any more. Soon she would not have to sing. The crowd looked at Oganda sympathetically, mumbling words she could not hear. But none of them pleaded for life. As Oganda opened the gate, a child, a young child, broke loose from the crowd, and ran towards her. The child took a small earring from her sweaty hands and gave it to Oganda saying, 'When you reach the world of the dead, give this earring to my sister. She died last week. She forgot this ring.' Oganda, taken aback by the strange request, took the little ring, and handed her precious water and food to the child. She did not need them now. Oganda did not know whether to laugh or cry. She had heard mourners sending their love to their sweethearts, long dead, but this idea of sending gifts was new to her.

Oganda held her breath as she crossed the barrier to enter the sacred land. She looked appealingly at the crowd, but there was no response. Their minds were too preoccupied with their own survival. Rain was the precious medicine they were looking for, and the sooner Oganda could get to her destination the better.

A strange feeling possessed Oganda as she picked her way in the sacred land. There were strange noises that often startled her, and her first reaction was to take to her heels. But she remembered that she had to fulfil the wish of her people. She was exhausted, but the path was still winding. Then suddenly the path ended on sandy land. The water had retreated miles away from the shore leaving a wide stretch of sand. Beyond this was the vast expanse of water.

Oganda felt afraid. She wanted to picture the size and shape of the monster, but fear would not let her. The society did not talk about it, nor did the crying children who were silenced by the mention of its name. The sun was still up, but it was no longer hot. For a long time Oganda walked ankle-deep in the sand. She was exhausted and longed desperately for her calabash of water. As she moved on, she had a strange feeling that something was following her. Was it the monster? Her hair stood erect, and a cold paralysing feeling ran along her spine. She looked behind, sideways and in front, but there was nothing, except a cloud of dust.

Oganda pulled up and hurried but the feeling did not leave her, and her whole body became saturated with perspiration.

The sun was going down fast and the lake shore seemed to move along with it.

Oganda started to run. She must be at the lake before sunset. As she ran she heard a noise coming from behind. She looked back sharply, and something resembling a moving bush was frantically running after her. It was about to catch up with her.

Oganda ran with all her strength. She was now deter-mined to throw herself into the water even before sunset. She did not look back, but the creature was upon her. She made an effort to cry out, as in a nightmare, but she could not hear her own voice. The creature caught up with Oganda. In the utter confusion, as Oganda came face to face with the unidentified creature, a strong hand grabbed her. But she fell flat on the sand and fainted.

When the lake breeze brought her back to consciousness, a man was bending over her. '........!' Oganda opened her mouth to speak, but she had lost her voice. She swallowed a mouthful of water poured into her mouth by the stranger.

'Osinda, Osinda! Please let me die. Let me run, the sun is going down. Let me die, let them have rain.' Osinda fondled the glittering chain around Oganda's waist and wiped the tears from her face.

'What must escape quickly to the unknown land,' Osinda said urgently. 'We must run away from the wrath of the ancestors and the retaliation of the monster.'

'But the curse is upon me, Osinda, I am no good to you any more. And moreover the eyes of the ancestors will follow us everywhere and bad luck will befall us. Nor can we escape from the monster.'

Oganda broke loose, afraid to escape, but Osinda grabbed her hands again.

'Listen to me, Oganda! Listen! Here are two coats!' He then covered the whole of Oganda's body, except her eyes, with a leafy attire made from the twigs of *Bwombwe*. 'These will protect us from the eyes of the ancestors and the wrath of the monster. Now let us run out of here.' He held Oganda's hand and they ran from the sacred land, avoiding the path that Oganda had followed.

The bush was thick, and the long grass entangled

their feet as they ran. Halfway through the sacred land they stopped and looked back. The sun was almost touching the surface of the water. They were frightened. They continued to run, now faster, to avoid the sinking sun.

'Have faith, Oganda – that thing will not reach us.'

When they reached the barrier and looked behind them trembling, only a tip of the sun could be seen above the water's surface.

'It is gone! It is gone!' Oganda wept, hiding her face in her hands.

'Weep not, daughter of the chief. Let us run, let us escape.'

There was a bright lightning. They looked up, frightened. Above them black furious clouds started to gather. They began to run. Then the thunder roared, and the rain came down in torrents.

Study activities

....

The Late Bud (Ghana)

1 With partners, discuss and jot down your responses to the following:

a) From whose point of view is the story being told?

b) How, according to her mother, was Yaaba being difficult and disobedient?

c) Do you think the mother was justified in treating Yaaba differently from the other children? Explain your views.

d) With whom would you say the author's sympathy lies – with Yaaba, her mother, or both equally? Argue your case.

2 With which of the following statements about this story by Ama Ata Aidoo would you agree?

a) 'The story is about a sad misunderstanding between a child and her mother.'

b) 'The story is about learning to share domestic work.'

c) 'The story is about a parent struggling to bring up a difficult child.'

d) 'The story suggests that parents like obedient children!' (See the quotation at the start of the story.)

e) 'The story is about love and reconciliation.'

3 Continue the story from where it stops. You may like to focus on how Yaaba and her mother restore good relations.

4 Choose an important part of the story and rewrite it from the mother's point of view.

Marriage is a Private Affair (Nigeria)

1 Chinua Achebe writes as an outsider, one who observes the characters and events from a distance. Does this suggest that he sympathises with Nene, Nnaemeka and his father equally? Argue your views.

2 With whom do you feel the greatest sympathy? Explain your views.

3 What finally causes a change of heart for the elderly father? Explain in detail.

4 Imagine Nnaemeka's father decides at last to write a long letter in reply to Nene and Nnaemeka. His tone and manner this time will be quite different. Write this letter. (You will find it useful to reread the last few pages of the story, starting at: 'It amazes me that you could be so unfeeling . . .'.)

5 Describe the occasion when the family finally come together after years of separation. Remember: Nene and her children will meet Nnaemeka's father for the first time.

The Ivory Dancer (Nigeria)

1 This story by Cyprian Ekwensi reveals a conflict between Akunma's private promise to Peters and her public duty to dance for the benefit of her village community. In refusing to dance, Akunma takes several risks. What are these? Was she right to take these risks? Explain your views.

2 The story shows how different characters make different sacrifices. What sacrifices were made by Akunma, Chibo and the village chief? Is there any irony in any of these sacrifices?

3 With whom do you feel greater sympathy – Akunma or Chibo?

4 On the night of the dance, three important events occur:

- Peters betrays Akunma
- the chief's new young wife betrays him
- the village is promised a piped water supply.

Imagine the village chief and Akunma talking together the next day. Write out their conversation. You can bring Chibo into this if you wish to.

5 Everyone enjoys a love story. Can you write a good one?

A Man Can Try (Sierra Leone)

1 In revealing Marie's thoughts, Eldred Durosimi Jones tells us (paragraph three): 'She had known from the first that this moment [of parting] would come. In their type of relationship, parting was as inevitable as death . . .' What 'type of relationship' did Tullock have with Marie? How happy do you think they were together?

2 Reread paragraphs five and six of the story (beginning with: 'He, too, had been happy with Marie . . .').

a) What is your response to Prothero's advice to Tullock?

b) How is Tullock influenced by this advice? Was it inevitable that Tullock should 'desert' Marie, as we are told earlier in the story?

3 In the first paragraph of the story, the local African chief says:

- to Tullock: 'I really do not see how anyone could have been fairer than you have been . . .'; and
- to Marie: 'You should count yourself lucky to have had D. C. Tullock for your husband.'

Would you agree with these views? Argue your case.

4 How are Marie and Denise different?

5 We are told Denise had strong views about 'the rights of women'. How do you think she would feel about Tullock's treatment of Marie?

6 Tullock has doubts about marrying Denise. But 'he brushed the question aside. It did not matter. He had to.' Do you think they will be happy together? Explain your views.

7 Do you think Tullock will adjust to life in England? How was his life in Africa different?

8 Imagine that Tambah (Tullock's son) has become educated with money his father has been sending to Marie. Tambah, as a young man, decides to visit Tullock and Denise in England. Write a story about the day the visit occurs.

Ding Dong Bell (Ghana)

Residents of a village community without piped water supply would have to walk (or bicycle) considerable distances to fetch fresh water for use at home. Having wells in their village compound would clearly be very convenient, especially for the women who have to carry the water. (Five litres of water weigh over 5 kg.)

1 What impressions of village life do you get from the first six paragraphs of this story by Kwabena Annan? Jot down notes about their housing, roads, schooling, water supply, relations with neighbouring villages, their life-style generally, and how they feel about outsiders who suggest change.

2 Reread paragraph seven, beginning with 'Well, I could have told him straight away . . .'. According to the story-teller, how do the village people feel about their government in Accra and the European who has come to talk to them about 'development'?

3 Which of the following statements would you agree with? The story is about:

a) tradition versus change;

b) admired leadership of a village community;

c) a happy community that want a hassle-free life;

d) Government versus the people;

e) complacency;

f) (give your own suggestions).

4 Instead of outsiders, imagine it is the village women who challenge the village men about the urgent need for freshwater wells. Write about this debate in playscript form, or organise a formal debate in your class.

136

5 Rewrite the story from the viewpoint of the European Government Agent. You may like to begin with his impressions of this village community as he arrives on a Thursday, when the villagers are relaxing with *'akpeteshie . . .'*. Will your story be amusing, as is the original?

The Answer is No (Egypt)

1 The woman in this story by Naguib Mahfouz remains single despite many offers of marriage. Which of the following do you consider explains her decision?

a) When fourteen, she was sexually abused by a private tutor whom she had trusted as a father figure.

b) In an Islamic country, the loss of her virginity before marriage means she would be unacceptable as a marriage partner to all men other than her abuser. The author tells us: 'She had either to accept or to close the door for ever.'

c) She had developed a fear of love (see the last part of the story).

d) She could not be sure whether the men offering to marry her were keen on her or only on her money.

e) She valued her 'personal independence' too much to risk giving it up.

f) She felt marriage would mean an unequal partnership. Why does the young woman reject the man when he returns with a proposal of marriage?

2 What are your views of the man who was once the girl's private tutor and is now her headteacher?

3 Imagine the woman keeps a personal diary. Write out in detail her thoughts and feelings at the end of the first school day, having met the new headteacher.

4 Imagine *she* is the headteacher at the school where he wants to apply for a job as a teacher. Describe what happens when he visits her to gather information about the school.

Another Evening at the Club (Egypt)

1 In this story by Alifa Rifaat, what were the reasons why Samia's parents were pleased to have Abboud-Bey as a husband for their daughter?

2 Before her marriage to Abboud-Bey, Samia's mother had told her: 'You're a lucky girl. He's a real find. Any girl would be happy to have him.' Looking back on her marriage, do you think Samia considers herself lucky? Do *you* think she is lucky and happy? Explain your views.

3 Imagine that Samia writes a letter explaining the incident about the ring to her mother. Write this letter. Try to show how Samia feels about the way her husband handled the situation, the way he treated Samia and Gazia and whether she feels 'lucky' and 'happy' to be his wife.

4 Imagine that the police ask Abboud-Bey to prosecute Gazia over the 'theft' of the ring, and that she is defended by a very smart lawyer paid for by the government. Abboud-Bey will be the plaintiff, Gazia the defendant, and Samia the key witness. Describe the trial.

The Story of the Chest (Algeria)

1 Towards the end of the story, the author, Marguerite Amrouche, tells us: 'Now they understood one another.' Describe in what ways this is so.

2 What would you say *The Story of the Chest* is about? Is it:

a) about a *prince* who values his wife for her cleverness, up to a point?

b) about a *man* who does not feel threatened by his wife's cleverness?

c) about a marriage of unequal partners whose relationship becomes equal through love, respect and honour?

b) that what matters in a relationship is not who is cleverer, but whether it is based on love?

e) a love story?

3 Because this story is a fable, it may seem unrealistic. In what details does it seem imaginary to you? You may find it helpful to jot down notes under headings such as: characters, events, the choice of language, dialogue, setting etc.

4 Using the above notes, rewrite this story so that it seems true to life.

No Witchcraft for Sale (Zimbabwe)

1 This story by Doris Lessing shows various ways in which white people – as individuals, as families, and as a community – depend on their black servants. Describe as many as you can.

2 Looking back over the first five paragraphs of the story, how would you describe the relationship between Gideon and little Teddy? Father and son? Childminder and child? A sort of friendship? Give reasons for your choice of answer. Why is it that we do not hear of Gideon playing with his own son?

3 Mrs Farquar agrees with Gideon that when their children grow up, Teddy will become a 'baas' while Gideon's son will become a servant. Gideon, who attended a mission school, was taught to believe that this was 'God's will'. What is meant by this phrase, and how does it affect the lives of these characters?

4 We gather that Gideon had learnt his medical wisdom from his elders when young. Imagine that in his old age, Gideon plans to pass on his wisdom to his son. He begins by explaining how he once saved Teddy's life, how the Farquars and the scientist had put pressure on him to hand over his expertise, and why he felt so strongly about not revealing it. Imagine and write out this conversation.

The Advance (Congo)

1 In this story by Henry Lopes, what impressions do you have of Madam, Carmen's employer? Select evidence from the story of her role as a mother, an employer, and generally in her attitude to people who have to work as servants.

2 Carmen considered bringing her son to Madam's house. Why didn't she do so?

3 Madam blames Carmen for not saving regularly. Was this possible? Explain as fully as possible, including the details of Carmen's monthly income.

4 Who do you think is to blame for the death of Carmen's son – Carmen, her poverty, Madam, or just a combination of circumstances? Explain your views.

5 Compare and contrast Madam and Carmen as mothers. What conclusions do you draw?

6 On a previous occasion when Carmen had attended a funeral, Madam had warned her against taking more time off work. Imagine Carmen does take a day off for her son's funeral. Imagine what would happen when she returns to work the following day, and describe the scene.

The Ultimate Safari (South Africa)

The Swahili word 'safari' means a journey or an expedition; in East Africa it can also mean a journey by car through the safari parks to see wildlife.

1 Having read the story, think of possible reasons why the author, Nadine Gordimer, chose to begin with the quotation from an advertisement. Decide from the following suggestions which one(s) you would agree with:

a) to show that for the black families in the story the 'safari' was a journey of survival, forced by war;

b) to show that the travelling families were on a journey of adventure through Kruger Safari Park;

c) to show the difference of experience between well-off tourists who travel in cars to see wildlife and desperate refugees whose lives are at risk walking through a safari park;

d) to suggest irony in the title of the story.

2 What impression do you have about the character of the grandmother? Select evidence from the story to support your views.

3 What do you think happened to the grandfather? In your view was the grandmother right to keep up with the rest of the refugees when her husband failed to turn up? Explain your answer.

4 The story reveals a series of sacrifices made by various people, particularly the grandmother. What were these? What is your response to them?

5 The child who tells the story feels, at the end, that there is a home for her to return to, while her grandmother says that for them: 'There is nothing. No home.' Which of them is right? Should the child be allowed to discover the truth, or should her grandmother stop her from making the journey to find out? Give reasons for your views.

6 Imagine that you are a journalist and that you are asked to write the leading article for a newspaper about what happened to the child story-teller's family. Write this piece, using any other information you come across.

Kgotla (South Africa)

1 According to you, who was really responsible for the trouble that started in Gobosamang's family? Choose one or more from the following suggestions (you may make up your own too):

- the villagers: they 'decided to poison this happy marriage because they were wild with jealousy' of Rose's beauty
- Rose: she was an unacceptable 'foreigner'
- Gobosamang: he was described as 'a senseless man' by Thatayarona and he was jealous of Rose because he was blind.

2 Kelapile, one of the village elders who advises the parties at dispute, reminds all what their forefathers had said: 'Jealousy starts from the eye.' Does this mean that even if Gobosamang was sighted, the troubles would still have arisen? Explain your answer.

3 Were the village elders right to fine Tsietso for assaulting Gobosamang's elderly mother? Explain your answer.

4 Rose offers to repay Tsietso for all that Tsietso lost when with Gobosamang. What is your response to this?

5 With whom do you have greater sympathy – Rose or Tsietso? Explain your views.

6 Near the beginning of the story we are told that the modern government in South Africa is gradually taking over all the work that has so far been carried out by the kgotla, an informal village 'court' that is run free of charge by the elders who are respected for their wisdom in their village community. Do you think the dispute was better settled at the kgotla or would it be better in a modern court of law? Write a short piece in which you argue the case for and against keeping the kgotla.

The Return (Kenya)

The Mau Mau movement was an uprising against British rule in Kenya in the 1950s. It occurred mainly because the black communities there were angry about the confiscation of their land and their long-standing grievances were ignored. The Gikuyu, a large ethnic group, were among those who rebelled. Eleven thousand rebels were killed and up to eighty thousand Gikuyu men, women and children were confined in detention camps.

1 As he walks home after release from a detention camp, Kamau has high hopes and expectations about the way he will be received by his people. What are these?

2 As he gets closer to home, Kamau meets a series of deep disappointments. Describe these.

3 Look again at the fourth paragraph of this story by Ngugi Wa Thiong'o. Why did Kamau feel he might receive a 'hero's welcome' home?

4 After listening to his mother, Kamau feels angry and betrayed. By whom and in what way?

5 Reread the last paragraph of the story. Kamau was held in detention for five years without trial. What gave him the mental strength to survive this very stressful experience?

6 Why does Kamau not try to rescue the bundle which he watches floating away down the river? What does the bundle symbolise?

7 What is your response to the last three sentences of the story (from 'Thoughts of drowning . . .')? What do they reveal about Kamau's character?

The Rain Came (Kenya)

1 The second paragraph of this story by Grace Ogot tells us that the village community were increasingly desperate about the shortage of water, but they had faith in their chief to help them. How does this affect him?

2 In paragraph six, we are told: 'Refusing to yield to the rainmaker's request would mean sacrificing the whole tribe, putting the interests of the individual above those of the society.' Labong'o decides to try and save his people. What does this tell us about him? How will the loss of his daughter affect him?

3 What thoughts and feelings go through the mind of Minya, Oganda's mother, after the chief has announced the decision that their daughter must die?

4 Oganda thinks the village community are happy because her marriage is to occur soon. In fact, they rejoice because they think her sacrifice will bring rain. How does Oganda feel about her community when she discovers why they are celebrating? What is your reaction to the community?

5 How is the last paragraph of the story significant?

6 When making his speech to his people, the chief was too upset to say very much. Write about the occasion, including the *whole* of his speech, as well as the reaction of the audience as he proceeds. Will he speak both as a brave leader as well as a grieving father?

The authors

Chinua Achebe (1930–) was born in Nigeria and is, in addition to Wole Soyinka, perhaps the most widely known of African writers. He went to university in Nigeria and has published poetry, novels and short stories. He was also general editor of the Heinemann African Writers Series. *Marriage is a Private Affair* comes from *Girls at War and Other Stories* (Heinemann, 1972). His novels include *Things Fall Apart* (1958), *No Longer at Ease* (1960), *Arrow of God* (1964) and *Anthills of the Savanna* (1987), which was short-listed for the important Booker Prize.

Ama Ata Aidoo (1942–) was born and educated in Ghana. She writes poetry, drama and novels as well as short stories. In recent years she has been involved in Ghanaian politics and has also spent time writing and studying in the USA. *The Late Bud* comes from *No Sweetness Here* (Longman African Classics, 1970). Her other works include *Our Sister Killjoy* (1977), a novel, and *The Dilemma of a Ghost* (1964) and *Anowa* (1969), both plays.

Marguerite Amrouche (1913–76) was born in North Africa and after her education in Spain settled in France. She wrote three novels. She was also a well-known folklorist and she translated into French a collection of Kabyle proverbs, tales, lyrics and chants that her mother had taught her.

Kwabena Annan was born in Ghana. He was a civil servant for many years. It has not been possible to find out more about him.

Cyprian Ekwensi (1921–) was born in Nigeria and attended universities in Nigeria and London, where he qualified in pharmacy. He has worked as a science teacher, broadcaster, civil servant and pharmacist and is now retired and living in Nigeria. His second and probably most widely known and influential novel is *Jagua Nana* (1961). *The Ivory Dancer* is from his collection of stories *Lokotown and Other Stories* (1966). He has published a further collection of short stories called *Restless City and Christmas Gold* (1975).

Nadine Gordimer (1923–) was born in South Africa, went to university in Johannesburg, where her home now is and which is the setting for most of her fiction. Her work was banned in South Africa for some time because of her political views. She has published over twenty books and is one of South Africa's best-known writers. She shared the Booker Prize for her novel *The Conservationist* (1974) and won the Nobel Prize for Literature in 1991. Her other novels include *The Lying Days* (1953), *A Guest of Honour* (1970), and *Burger's Daughter* (1979).

Bessie Head (1937–86) was born in Pietermaritzburg, in eastern South Africa, the 'coloured' child of a white woman. She spent her childhood in a foster home, then attended a mission school and trained as a teacher. She went on to work as a teacher and journalist, before deciding to go into exile in neighbouring Botswana in 1963. Her three novels, *When Rain Clouds Gather* (1968), *Maru* (1971) and *A Question of Power* (1973), are set in her adopted country. The story *Kgotla* appears in *The Collector of Treasures* (Heinemann African Writers Series, 1977). This was followed by her historic portrait of the town in Botswana where she lived, called *Serowe: Village of the Rain Wind* (1981).

Eldred Durosimi Jones (1925–) was born in Sierra Leone and completed his education at Oxford. From 1953 until his retirement he was a teacher at Fourah Bay College, Freetown, which he had himself attended. He has published several academic books and is editor of an annual review of African literature called *African Literature Today*.

Doris Lessing (1919–) was born in Iran of British parents and spent her childhood on a farm in Southern Rhodesia, now Zimbabwe. She moved to England in 1949. By then she had written her first novel *The Grass is Singing* (published in 1950). She has written over twenty-five books, including five collections of short stories, essays and reviews. Among her novels are *The Golden Notebook* (1962), *The Summer Before the Dark* (1973) and *The Good Terrorist* (1985).

Henry Lopes (1937–) was born in Kinshasa in Zaire, where he lived for twelve years, and then moved to France. At university in France he studied history and went on to teach at a college in Brazzaville in the Congo. His teaching career was soon interrupted when he was made Minister of Education and, later, Prime Minister. His works include poetry and three novels, but the short-story collection *Tribaliks* (Heinemann African Writers Series, 1987), from which the story *The Advance* is taken, is the only one translated into English. He now works in Paris for UNESCO.

Naguib Mahfouz (1911–) was born in Cairo and attended Cairo University where he studied philosophy. He is the most renowned novelist of the Arab world and won the Nobel Prize for Literature in 1988. He has written more than thirty novels, with *Midaq Alley* (1947), one of his earliest books, still a bestseller in Egypt. The *Answer Is No* comes from *The Time and the Place and Other Stories* (Doubleday, 1992).

Grace Ogot (1930–) was born in Kenya where she grew up and now lives. She trained as a midwife in Uganda and England and has worked as a nurse and midwifery tutor and also as a BBC Radio Announcer, a newspaper columnist and a Community Development Officer. She is an outstanding story-teller and the story *The Rain Came*, told to her by her grandmother, is from *Land Without Thunder* (East African Publishing House, 1968). She has also written several novels including *The Promised Land* (1966) and a second collection of short stories called *The Island of Tears* (1980).

Alifa Rifaat (1930–) was born and grew up in Egypt as part of a 'traditional' Egyptian family. As the wife of a police officer, she has spent most of her adult life in different parts of Egypt and now lives in Cairo. Her two collections of short stories are published under the title *Distant View of a Minaret* (Heinemann African Writers Series, 1987).

Ngugi Wa Thiong'o (1938–) was born in Limuru, Kenya, of a peasant family. He got his degree in English in Uganda and followed this with further study in England at the University of Leeds. He then taught at the University of Nairobi. A short while after his play *I Will Marry When I Want* (1982) was staged in Gikuyu in his hometown of Limuru, Ngugi was arrested and then detained without trial for a year. After his release he was forced into exile in Europe and has lived outside Kenya, including in London, for some time. His first novel *Weep Not Child* (1964) was the first novel from East Africa to be published in English. He is East Africa's best-known writer and his other work includes *A Grain of Wheat* (1967), *Petals of Blood* (1977) and the short-story collection *Secret Lives* (Heinemann African Writers Series, 1975).

Further reading

Collections

Unwinding Threads: Writing by Women in Africa edited by
Charlotte Bruner (Heinemann, 1983)
A fine collection with very helpful introductions to each
region and author included.

A Land Apart: A South African Reader edited by André Brink
and J.M. Coetzee (Faber, 1986)
This strong and bold selection of prose and poetry reflects
the tensions and stresses of a divided South Africa.

Girls at War and Other Stories by Chinua Achebe
(Heinemann, 1972)
The first collection of short stories by this famous author.

The Heinemann Book of Contemporary African Short Stories
edited by Chinua Achebe and C.L. Innes (1992)
An anthology that spans the length and breadth of Africa
and includes famous as well as new writers.

No Sweetness Here by Ama Ata Aidoo (Longman, 1970)
A beautifully written set of stories by one of Africa's leading
writers.

Crimes of Conscience by Nadine Gordimer (Heinemann,
1991) and *Some Monday For Sure* (Heinemann, 1976)
The second of these fine sets of stories is a personal
selection by the author from stories she published over
twenty-five years, and they reflect the socio-political
changes in South Africa over that period.

The Collector of Treasures by Bessie Head (Heinemann, 1977) and *Tales of Tenderness and Power* (Heinemann, 1990)
Stories by one of the most accomplished writers from South Africa.

We Killed Mangy Dog and other Mozambique Stories by Luis Bernardo Honwana (Heinemann, 1969)
Readers may wish to try the title story to sample Honwana's style.

Secret Lives by Ngugi Wa Thiong'o (Heinemann, 1975)
A collection that in a sense reflects the author's 'creative autobiography', as he puts it, and includes some fine stories.

Soweto Stories by Miriam Tlali (Pandora Press, 1989)
A collection from one of South Africa's highly regarded authors.

Opening the Gates: A Century of Arab Feminist Writing edited by Margot Badran and Miriam Cooke (Virago, 1990)
A diverse collection that includes letters, memoirs, speeches, fiction and poetry by women from over twenty states.

Books on African writing

African Literatures in the Twentieth Century: A Guide edited by Leonard S. Klein (Oldcastle Books, 1988)
A helpful book: thirty-eight African countries and forty-three authors are represented including many famous ones, but with a bias towards male writers.

Female Novelists of Modern Africa by Oladele Taiwo
(Macmillan, 1984)
An important study of a selection of works by authors that
include Miriama Ba, Ama Ata Aidoo, Flora Nwapa, Bucchi
Emecheta, Grace Ogot, Miriam Tlali and Bessie Head.

In Their Own Voices: African Women Writers Talk edited by
Adeola James (Heinemann,1990)
A valuable series of interviews with well-known as well as
aspiring writers mainly from West and East Africa that raise
a whole range of issues including the role of African women
in literature and society.

Writers from Africa by Stewart Brown (The Book Trust, 1989)
An extremely useful brief guide to many African authors
across the whole of Africa.

*Wasafiri: Caribbean, African, Asian and Associated Literatures
in English* edited by Susheila Nasta
A highly acclaimed and stimulating literary magazine with a
growing international reputation. (To subscribe, write to
The Editor, Wasafiri, Dept of English, Queen Mary and
Westfield College, University of London, Mile End Road,
London E1 4NS.)

History

A Short History of Africa by Roland Oliver and J.D. Fage
(Penguin, 6th edition 1988)